THE MAN OF BRONZE

Doc Savage was much better known than he would have liked to be.

The natural hue of his skin was a deep bronze, the product of exposure to tropical suns—the fact that his hair was a bronze color only slightly darker gave him a striking aspect.

Newspaper and magazine articles had publicized him as that strange and remarkable individual who made a business of righting wrongs and punishing evildoers who happened to be outside the law.

Bantam Books by Kenneth Robeson
Ask your bookseller for the books you have missed

About Doc Savage
   DOC SAVAGE: HIS APOCALYPTIC LIFE
     by Philip José Farmer

THE
BOSS OF
TERROR

A DOC SAVAGE® ADVENTURE

BY KENNETH ROBESON

THE BOSS OF TERROR
*A Bantam Book / published by arrangement with
The Condé Nast Publications Inc.*

PRINTING HISTORY
Originally published in DOC SAVAGE Magazine May 1940
Bantam edition / November 1976

ISBN 0-553-06424-X

Published simultaneously in the United States and Canada

*Bantam Books are published by Bantam Books, Inc. Its trade-
mark, consisting of the words "Bantam Books" and the por-
trayal of a bantam, is registered in the United States Patent
Office and in other countries. Marca Registrada. Bantam
Books, Inc., 666 Fifth Avenue, New York, New York 10019.*

CONTENTS

Chapter I

THE LOONS

The ambulance was traveling about fifty when it took a corner and missed a lamp-post scarcely more than a quarter of an inch.

The passenger spoke to the driver.

"The stork that brought you," he said, "should have been arrested for smuggling dope."

The driver grinned. He looked startlingly like an ape when he grinned—and before he grinned, for that matter.

The ambulance lined out on a straight stretch through the park and the speedometer climbed up to seventy. The siren made a lot of cat-on-the-fence noise.

The passenger—he rode in the front seat with the driver—was wasp-waisted and wide-shouldered, with an orator's mouth. He wore striped afternoon trousers, a cut-away coat, a pearl-colored vest. In other words, he was dressed fit to kill. He balanced a neat black cane on his knees.

The driver yanked the wheel. The ambulance took a corner on two wheels, tires howling in complaint.

"From the way you drive this ambulance," the passenger said, "one would think you owned it."

The driver snorted. "Well," he said, "nobody knows we stole it—yet."

Nothing more was said for some time. The ambulance dived out of Central Park, which occupies the middle part of New York City like a great lung, and veered sharply north on the street that runs along the west side of the park, Central Park West.

The driver came near being as wide as he was tall. Standing on his feet, he could scratch his knees with his fingers without bending over. There was a good deal of reddish hair, of the nature of rusty shingle nails, on all exposed parts of his person. His face was something to frighten babies with; yet babies usually weren't frightened by him. There was something pleasantly fascinating about his homeliness.

The driver pointed with one hand. "Isn't that it?" he asked.

He was indicating a limousine—a long black limousine that looked like at least seven thousand dollars recently invested. It was empty, except for the chauffeur.

"That's it," the dapper man admitted.

"Sure it's it," said the driver. "I told you we could head it off by cutting through the park."

"The way you've been driving," complained the other, "you could have headed off Eddie Rickenbacker in an airplane."

This seemed to enrage the ambulance driver. He gave the wheel a jerk. The ambulance crashed into the limousine. There was a great deal of noise.

There was more noise than damage, really, although there was some shock, too—enough to pile ambulance driver and passenger against the windshield, and enough to knock the uniform cap off the limousine driver.

The driver got out of the limousine obviously with just one intention, which was to fight. He looked as if he could give an account of himself, being practically seven feet tall and built along the symmetrical proportions of a circus acrobat. It was a case of no particular part of him being big—he was *all* big. He jerked open the ambulance door.

"Come out of there, you mutts!" he ordered angrily.

The ambulance driver and his dapper companion sat perfectly still, glancing at each other out of the corners of their eyes, but not saying anything.

"Come out!" The giant limousine driver grabbed the

ambulance door and shook it—shook the whole ambulance. "Come out, you skulls!" he bellowed. "I'm gonna ruin you both!"

From the corner of his mouth, the dapper man whispered, "Gosh, he's big, isn't he?"

Also from the side of his mouth, the ambulance driver agreed, "He wants to play rough, too."

"So you won't come out, eh?" roared the limousine pilot. "O.K. I'll take you out."

He reached in and got the dapper passenger by one leg. The well-dressed man yelled, "Wait, you fool! I wasn't driving this thing!" This remonstration did no good; he was dragged out anyway. "Run into me, will you!" said the giant. He knocked the dapper man flat on his back in the street. He said, "That'll teach you." He reached in and grabbed the apish man by the leg.

"Now wait a minute," said the apish man hastily. "Let's talk this thing over."

"Talk, hell! You ran into me. What's there to talk about?"

"People run into other people every day. What's there to argue—"

"They don't run into them on purpose. Not into me, anyway."

The limousine chauffeur then hit the ambulance driver with his fist. The ambulance driver staggered, but not as much as might have been expected. He emitted a howl, the noise being somewhat like the sound made by a bull when one of his horns is being sawed off by a cowboy.

A fight ensued. If the street had not been paved with asphalt, the brawl would doubtless have raised quite a cloud of dust. Soon the big limousine chauffeur hit the pavement alongside the dapper ambulance passenger, and sat there, his breath temporarily knocked out.

"Hit him, Ham!" puffed the apish ambulance driver.

"Nothing doing," said the dapper man. "He might hit back."

"Fine help you are!" said the apish man. He took in a deep breath, then rushed his dazed opponent. He received a left hook between the eyes that made him stagger back. He rushed again. This time, he clipped the big limousine chauffeur on the jaw, dazing him and knocking him down.

"Nice going, Monk," said the dapper Ham. "Too bad you didn't have a sledge hammer."

The apish Monk puffed for breath and surveyed the size of his momentarily stupefied opponent.

"I know what elephant hunters feel like now," he remarked.

The dapper man nodded.

"You'll know what a hamburger feels like—if he gets up once more," he said. "I don't believe you can knock him down again."

"Help me throw him in the back of the ambulance," Monk ordered.

"Not me. He's your bird."

"Give me a hand, or I'll ram that cane down your throat."

The apish man and the dapper man laid hold of the arms of the limousine driver. The latter was still dazed, but he could get words out, after a fashion.

"What're you gonna do?" he gasped, trying to struggle.

"Why, we're going to give you a loving kiss," Monk said.

They heaved the big limousine chauffeur into the back of the ambulance and locked the doors.

A policeman arrived.

The cop had seen the whole thing, but it happened that he, as an individual, did not hold any excessive love for either ambulance drivers or the pilots of extremely swanky and shiny limousines, so he had remained in the background. He thought the thing was rather evenly matched. He liked a good fight. But now he thought he'd better stop it.

"Hey, you!" he barked. "What's going on here?"

Monk and Ham glanced at each other. The glances were not happy.

"There was an accident," Monk said.

"Yes," Ham added. "And we came to get the injured man. We just put him in the ambulance."

"You're not kidding me," the officer said. "I saw the whole thing."

He was a large, square officer, general color reddish. He looked as if he might have been partially constructed of the roots of oak trees. He was twirling a club almost as long as his arm. There was a noticeable bulge under one of his coat tails that was probably a revolver.

"It was this way, officer," said Monk, moved by inspiration. "The poor fellow is demented. His mind has been affected. Probably it is the heat—"

"It's been cold for a week," the officer said.

"The heat of nervous strain," said Monk, "caused by driving in this New York traffic. At any rate, his mind isn't right. We were going to take him to the hospital for observation."

Ham nodded emphatically. "Yes, that's it. We think he should be observed."

"He's worth observing," the cop said. "Particularly, the way he swings a right hook."

"His mind—"

"There's nothing wrong with his mind," the policeman growled. "Anybody would get mad the way you two fellows ran into his car. Probably his boss will give him hell."

Monk and Ham looked hurt.

"Officer, I'm afraid you don't believe us," Ham muttered.

At this point, there was a violent beating on the rear doors of the ambulance.

"Let me out of here!" a voice squalled.

The cop twirled his club ominously and scowled at Monk and Ham.

"Turn him loose," he ordered.

"But—"

"Turn him loose!" The policeman fished out a pair of handcuffs. "The Clancys don't tell you twice. Either you turn him loose, or—" He twirled the bracelets suggestively.

"I'll let him out," Monk said with haste.

"And I'll get ready to run," Ham said uneasily.

Monk unlocked the rear doors. The limousine chauffeur stumbled out onto the pavement. One of his eyes had turned black—it was remarkably black, considering the short time that had elapsed—and there was some damp red fluid on his fists, as if he had skinned them. He appeared mad enough to give off sparks.

"You want to prefer charges against these two?" the policeman asked him hopefully.

"I'll get 'em!" the driver growled ominously.

"You can have them arrested," the cop explained.

"Yes, and we can have him arrested, too," Ham said. "It's a horse of one color and a donkey of the same."

The officer scowled at Ham. "How come you know so much?"

"I'm a law—" Ham swallowed. "I studied law one time."

The limousine chauffeur blocked out his fists and glowered at Monk and Ham.

"I'll get you guys!" he said. "You just wait!"

Having rid himself of that threat, he stamped over and climbed into his machine.

"Hey!" called the cop. "Don't you want to prefer charges?"

"Go jump in the lake!" the chauffeur said.

The limousine had not been greatly damaged by the collision—there was a somewhat crumpled fender, but the wheels and the chassis were intact.

The chauffeur drove off in the limousine.

The cop stalked around to the back and looked into the ambulance, and started when he discovered a figure lying on a stretcher inside, swathed in white sheets.

"You got a patient in this thing!" he barked in astonishment.

"Oh, him," Monk said. "He's just an emergency case we was rushing to the hospital."

"Emergency case!" The cop looked blank. Then he gave Monk a poke with his billy club. "You idiot! Get in that thing and get going. The poor feller might have died while this tomfoolery was going on."

Monk and Ham climbed in the ambulance and disappeared up the street.

The cop stared after them. The cop was well satisfied with himself.

Of course, the officer was not aware that the present driver of the limousine was not the same chauffeur who had sat behind the wheel before the accident. There had been a change in limousine drivers.

Chapter II

THE HOUSE OF WORRIED FOLK

The limousine was composed about fifty percent of hood, the power plant being a sixteen-cylinder motor that was constructed with the care of a fine watch, or so the manufacturer claimed. It ran very quietly.

The chauffeur took the first opportunity to turn into a side street. He stopped. Producing a handkerchief and a small mirror, he repaired his appearance.

He wiped off the black eye. It was a smudge of dark grease paint.

He mopped up the red stains on his fists. These were a crimson-dyed sirup which did not leave permanent discoloration.

The next stop was at a place which made a specialty of quick body repairs.

"Had a little accident," the chauffeur explained. "Can you fix it up?"

He stood around while they put a thick coat of grease on the bent fender to keep the paint from cracking, then went to work with a small straightening machine and returned the fender to an appearance very close to its former one.

"Thanks," said the driver. "What do I owe you?"

"A dollar eighty— Say, you're sure a big guy, ain't you?"

"Yes." The driver paid up and drove the limousine to the home of John R. Smith, which was where it belonged. It was John R. Smith's limousine.

Out-of-town visitors to New York frequently walked along upper Fifth Avenue and mistook the John R.

Smith home for a museum, a bank, or even a modernistic church. Native New Yorkers often made the same error. It was a white marble edifice—"edifice" was the word—on the more swanky section of the Avenue.

The chauffeur drove into the garage. He inspected himself in the small mirror before he left the machine. The glass showed him a dark-skinned face, furry dark eyebrows, crow-black hair, and a scar—it was a long, thick scar that arched down from the corner of his left eye almost to the edge of his nose—which was his most distinguishing feature.

He made sure that the collodian compound out of which he had manufactured the scar was sticking tightly to his skin. Satisfied it was, he entered the house.

The interior of the house was a miniature of Grand Central Station—not so miniature, at that. It was a long way between pieces of furniture, and the furniture was huge.

It was a house full of strange-acting people. The chauffeur became aware of that by degrees, his first encounter being with the young woman who was walking backward.

The young woman came down a hallway. She was on her tiptoes; also she was moving backward. Her behavior seemed strange, almost eerie, for a moment; then the chauffeur realized she was retreating from someone and did not wish to be seen or heard.

The chauffeur reached out rather brazenly and took her arm. The young woman—it would have been natural for her to emit a frightened yelp, but she didn't —turned her head and looked at him coldly. She also moved one hand close to the large handbag she was carrying.

"What do *you* want?" she asked.

"I was afraid you might stumble," the chauffeur said mildly.

"Get out of this part of the house!" the young woman said. "You're a servant. You don't belong here."

She was a slender young woman with dark hair, charcoal-black eyes and a remarkably fine-textured skin of olive tint. It was almost as if her skin was made of silk. Her clothing—neat blue-serge street suit, high-heeled black Oxfords and a tricky little black hat—was obviously expensive. She was a completely smart person, and very much an eyeful.

"Do you belong here?" the chauffeur asked.

"What?"

"Do *you* belong here?"

"You insulting dog!" said the young woman. "I'll find John R. Smith and have you discharged."

The chauffeur grinned.

"I'll find John R. Smith and save you the trouble," he said. "I don't believe you belong in this house at all."

He walked away from the young woman with an air of determination. But he did not go far. He stopped around the nearest corner, and looked back cautiously.

The well-dressed young woman was in flight. She literally ran out through the front door and fled down the street.

The chauffeur accosted the butler, asking, "You let that girl in?"

"Why, yes."

"What name did she give?"

"Annie Spain, I believe. Yes—Annie Spain."

"Ever see her before?"

"No," said the butler, "I haven't."

"Then how come she got in?"

"The master," replied the butler stiffly, "seemed to be expecting her. He told me to show her in, which I did." The butler lost his formal manner, and inquired, "What the hell business is it of yours? You don't belong in this part of the house. Go back to the garage."

The chauffeur said, "Keep your shirt on," and walked away from the butler. But he did not return to the garage. Instead, he sauntered through the house. He carried his uniform cap in his hand, and seemed greatly interested in everything.

Finally he found the electrician.

The electrician was a rather scrawny-looking fellow who had a complexion that would have blended well with unbaked dough. He was standing on a chair in the west-wing library, tinkering with the mounted moose head that was over the fireplace—that is, he was doing this up until he heard the chauffeur coming. Then he gave a great jump and reached one of the air conditioning controls, with which he began to fumble.

The big chauffeur walked up and stood beside him.

"Is the moose head air-conditioned, too?" he asked.

"I was just looking at it," the electrician said. "Big one, ain't it? Good job of mounting, too."

Nothing was said for several moments, during which interval there was an air of stiffness in the room.

"Don't you recognize me, Long Tom?" the chauffeur asked suddenly.

The electrician gave a start, then stared unbelievingly.

"Good grief—no!" he exploded. "Say, that disguise is all right."

"It fooled the butler, so it seems that it might get by."

"I didn't know you."

The chauffeur pointed at the moose head. "What were you doing over there?"

"Rigging a microphone in the ear of the moose," Long Tom explained. "Makes a first-class spot for it. The ear of this moose was acoustically designed by nature for the purpose of picking up sound. With that microphone deep in the ear, and the wires run under the moose hair and through a hole in the wall—there's a closet nobody uses in the back, and I'm taking the lead-out through that—I should be able to make a phonograph recording of everything that anybody says in this room."

"Nobody suspects you?"

"Why should they? I'm supposed to be checking over the air-conditioning installation.

"How many rooms have you wired for eavesdropping?"

"About half of them. The ones they use the most. This is the last one I intend to wire."

The chauffeur was silent a moment. He might have been thinking.

"Do you know Annie Spain?" he asked abruptly.

"Who's she?" Long Tom shook his head. "No, I don't know anybody by that name."

"A very pretty dark-haired, dark-eyed girl who wears a blue tailored suit so plain that it must have cost two hundred dollars."

"I still don't know her."

"I see. Have you seen John R. Smith yet?"

"From a distance only."

"How is he?"

"Scared green," said Long Tom.

"Annie Spain is apparently well acquainted with John R. Smith," the chauffeur said thoughtfully.

The two men parted.

John R. Smith was one of the industrial powers of the United States—more properly, of the North and South Americas—and therefore frequently in trade magazines and confidential reports emanating from the New York and Buenos Aires stock exchanges, although on the other hand neither his pictures nor news about his personal doings were often seen in the daily newspapers, this last being true not so much because he was a modest man, but rather for the reason that too much newspaper publicity does very little for exceptionally rich men other than set them up as a target for moochers and skin-game artists. John R. Smith was certainly not modest. No man could be as rich as he had become and be truly modest. To get as much money as John R. Smith had, you needed to be convinced in your heart that you were a greater organizer than Napoleon and gifted with unparalleled courage.

John R. Smith was more often called Radiator Smith. Almost no one, except the people who worked for him, called him anything else. Persons in his employ were afraid to call him Radiator Smith.

But Radiator Smith he was. He was Radiator Smith in the John Smith Club to which he belonged. The John Smith Club had as members only men whose names were John Smith, and the John Smiths were designated with nicknames according to their professions—there was Insurance Smith, Bank Teller Smith, Broker Smith, Sailboat Smith, and a lot of other Smiths in the John Smith Club. John R. Smith was Radiator Smith because manufacturing radiators happened to be his principal business.

Radiators made in Radiator Smith's plant were used the world over in automobiles, airplanes, air-conditioning, and in whatever fashion radiators are employed.

Like many rich men, Radiator Smith had a no-good son. The son was named Maurice, and he and his father were the sole occupants—if one didn't count thirty-seven servants—of the huge mansion on upper Fifth Avenue. The other Smiths of the Radiator Smith clan had all passed on to the other world.

Radiator Smith liked to sit in royal privacy in the south-wing library—this library was larger than either the west-wing or the north-wing library, and more impressive—during his leisure at home. He made sure that he had one hour of leisure each day. He took it as he took his exercise, without fail.

Radiator Smith was sitting in the south-wing library with a cigar when the big chauffeur walked into his presence.

Radiator Smith jumped nervously. "What do you want?" he demanded.

"I just wanted to let you know we are on the job," the chauffeur said.

"Job?" Radiator Smith stared. "What job?"

"The one you called us in on."

"*What?*"

"You telephoned this morning. Surely you have not forgotten that soon."

"Say!" Radiator Smith sprang to his feet. "Who the devil are you?"

"Doc Savage," the chauffeur said.

Radiator Smith peered at the chauffeur. He rubbed his jaw, then scratched his head, giving an excellent picture of a man completely baffled.

"I never heard of you," he said. "Doc Savage—no, never heard of you."

A trace of a peculiar expression came over Doc Savage's features. "That's queer," he said.

In the house—not in this library, nor anywhere near it, but still somewhere in the house—there was a loud rap of a noise. Sharp. Somewhat like the sound of a shot, but not quite that either, because it was a longer noise. It did not have enough volume to excite either of the two men in the library, or distract their attention from each other.

The moneybags suddenly became irritated. He yelled, "What kind of a trick is this?"

"Don't start shouting," Doc Savage said quietly.

"Shout? I'll shout if I want to. Help! Police!" He ran for the door. "You're an intruder! I'm going to have you arrested!"

Just as Radiator Smith reached the library door, the door opened and the butler appeared. Radiator Smith collared the butler.

"Jonas!" he shouted. "Get the police!" He waved a hand over his shoulder at Doc Savage, explained, "We've got some kind of a crook here."

The butler, Jonas, made no move. He opened and shut his mouth, trying to speak. He was as pale as a regulation ghost is supposed to be, and had been that way when he opened the library door.

"Master Maurice," the butler finally managed to gasp. "Your son, sir."

"What about Maurice?"

"He just died, sir. Under—er—most peculiar circumstances."

Chapter III

THE QUEER DEATH

Radiator Smith had had a long career as a money-chaser during which he had ruined quite a number of men financially—those in close association with the radiator magnate had been known to whisper that at least four suicides marked the wake of Radiator Smith's activities in garnering one of the world's great fortunes—so the master of wealth should have been inured to shocks. But he didn't act like it now.

All of the muscles in his body seemed to jerk rigid and he made a coughing sound. He became pale slowly, then the paleness turned to a blue-green kind of hue. His breathing resolved into an unpleasant rattling noise, and he upset; he would have struck the floor quite heavily had Doc Savage not caught him.

Doc put the man in the handiest chair, began loosening his clothing at the tighter points.

"Get the medicine kit," Doc ordered.

"I'll call a doctor," the butler gasped.

"Get the medicine kit!" Doc said. "I'm a doctor."

The rattled butler yelled again, "I'll call a doctor!" and dashed out of the room.

The electrician—the man named Long Tom—dashed into the library, demanding, "Hey, what's going on? What ailed that butler?"

"He was going after a doctor," Doc explained.

"Doctor?" Long Tom stared. "Why, the damned fool! Don't he know that you're one of the world's leading physicians and surgeons?"

"He was excited," Doc said.

Long Tom pointed at Radiator Smith. "That's the money magnate himself—I've seen his pictures. What ails him?"

"Shock," Doc explained. "His machinery just stopped working. He will be all right in a moment—or at least he is not likely to die."

"It would be tough if he died," said Long Tom, "before he could tell us what kind of a mystery he wanted us to investigate."

"Something changed his mind."

"Eh?"

"He has decided he doesn't want us investigating," Doc explained. "Further than that, he seemed to want me completely out of the way—in jail."

A commotion was growing throughout the house, an uproar made by servants running and shouting to each other in alarmed voices.

"What's the fuss about?" Long Tom asked.

"The butler," Doc advised, "said something about Maurice Smith being dead."

"The old man's son?"

"Yes."

"From what I've heard, it's small loss," Long Tom said. "I'll go see." He ran out of the library.

Doc Savage worked over Radiator Smith. As a matter of fact, he was saving the wealthy man's life. The shock suffered had been paralytic in nature and almost complete, inducing a stoppage of heart function which would have been fatal without quick work—very skilled work, too, since there was no stimulating adrenalin or other chemicals immediately at hand.

Long Tom came back, almost flying. He was wild-eyed.

"This is the darnedest killing you ever heard of!" he exploded.

Doc said, "Block the doors. Let nobody in or out. Monk and Ham will be hanging around outside. Tell them to help watch the house."

"Will Monk and Ham be back yet?"

"They had to borrow that ambulance in a hurry—no time to rent or hire one. They were to return it at once so that they wouldn't be arrested as thieves. They should be back now."

"Right," Long Tom said, and vanished.

Doc Savage concluded it was safe to leave the financier for a few moments. He left the library, walked down the hall and passed two footmen who were carrying a maid. It appeared the maid had fainted.

Maurice Smith had been a long young man who carried a great deal of loose flesh on his body. Too much wine and song and not enough sleep and exercise had put pouches under his eyes that were nearly the size of tobacco sacks.

He was not in a pretty condition. His coat was ripped down the back and down one sleeve. Both of his shoes were off his feet and lying nearby—the shoes had not been unlaced; the laces had burst, as if a terrific force had wrenched off the shoes.

He sat in a chair—the chair was a huge thing with arms, so he had not fallen out—before a desk. The desk was a heavy one made of mahogany. The top was ripped across in a gigantic splinter-edged furrow which pointed toward Maurice Smith's body. A number of splinters from the top of the desk lay on the rich-looking rug.

The odor in the air was the most ugly thing in the room—probably it was the cause of the maid's fainting. It was the one smell that men never forget once they have encountered it—the odor of a burned man.

The room was a large one. Doc immediately noticed a difference from other rooms—the windows were triple; there were three windows in each opening, one outside another. Not two, as in the case of storm windows, but three. Also there were doors, and they were sealed with rubber around the edges.

"What kind of a room is this?" Doc asked.

The butler had come in, and he answered. "It is soundproofed," he said. "There are a number of soundproofed rooms in the house. That is to keep out the traffic noise of Fifth Avenue."

This Doc found to be the truth, so that the fact the room was soundproofed had no significance, other than it explained why the report heard earlier—the rap of a noise like a shot, but longer—had been no louder.

"I . . . I saw it huh—happen," the butler volunteered weakly.

"Saw what killed him, you mean?" Doc asked.

"It was lightning."

"Lightning?"

"Yes."

Doc Savage went to the windows—they were not open, nor could they be opened without tools. He could peer upward and see a patch of sky in which there were no clouds. He felt moved to voice an apparent fact.

"There couldn't have been any lightning," he said.

"It was lightning," the butler said. "It must have run into the room on something."

Doc Savage walked around the body. There was no life left in it, and no hope of bringing back any; he was sure of that. Furthermore, it did look like lightning.

"What makes you so sure it was lightning?" he asked the butler.

"I was almost struck by lightning once," the butler said. "I know how it is."

"When was that?"

"Ten years ago. No, eleven."

Doc made a wider tour of the room. He paused to moisten his fingers and carefully removed small colored-glass caps from his eyeballs. These caps had been the part of his disguise that made the color of his eyes dark, and they hampered vision somewhat. His eyes, after the caps were removed, showed a peculiar flake-gold color, and were almost hypnotically intense.

He paused and ran his fingers over the furniture. The furniture—the wooden parts of most of the pieces in the room—was coated with a thin layer of oil. But not all the furniture showed the film, he carefully noticed. He smelled the stuff. Shellac cut with alcohol; he concluded—the mixture that refinishers used to give old varnish new gloss.

"Long Tom!" he called.

Long Tom appeared. "Nobody in or out yet," he said. "The doors and windows are watched."

Doc said, "Will you go get Monk's portable chemical laboratory for me?"

"Sure."

Long Tom returned in a few minutes with the portable laboratory. The thing was contained in a case not as large as a small trunk, and while everything it held was on a miniature scale, it was almost fantastically complete. The homely Monk—he was one of the world's greatest industrial chemists, a fact that his apish looks belied—had lavished a great deal of careful work on creation of the laboratory, and he carried it around with him whenever he was working with Doc Savage.

Doc Savage went to work with the laboratory. He took samples first. Samples of the air, of the shattered desk top, of the dead man's clothing. He made tests, both with litmus paper and with chemical sprayings.

He was remarkably composed while he worked. If he found anything interesting, his expression gave no indication of the fact.

The butler had started staring at Doc Savage. He had discovered Doc was not the chauffeur; it had made him intensely suspicious.

"I'm going to call the police!" the butler barked suddenly.

"Why haven't you called them already?" Doc asked.

The butler looked surprised and sidled toward the telephone.

"Not that phone," Doc suggested. "There might be fingerprints."

The butler left the library.

Long Tom had been standing in the door. After the butler departed, the electrical expert moved over to Doc.

"That butler don't know who you are," Long Tom said. "Apparently Radiator Smith didn't tell anybody he'd called us in." The electrical wizard pointed at the dead man. "What killed him?"

"The butler thinks it was lightning."

Long Tom frowned. He had the reputation of being one of the most brilliant electrical experts who had developed in the decade since Steinmetz.

"Lightning," he said. "Where in the dickens would lightning come from? There's no lightning outside."

"That is one of the strange points."

"Well, it would have had to come from somewhere. People don't carry around lightning bolts and shoot 'em at other people like you shoot bullets. Therefore, it wasn't lightning."

"Take a look."

"Eh?"

"Examine the body."

With no taste for the job whatever, Long Tom began scrutinizing the corpse. But suddenly his interest became so aroused that he forgot his squeamishness.

"It *was* lightning!" he croaked.

"It was," Doc agreed, "according to every indication."

There was a commotion in the hall—a machine-gun rattle of footsteps, a rasping sound as the runner slid to make the turn into the room—and the homely Monk popped inside.

"Some guy makin' his getaway, Doc!" Monk exploded. "Takin' a sneak through a window!"

"You didn't seize him?"

"Thought you might want to follow him," Monk said.

"Nice idea. You fellows stay here and explain to the police."

"But how'll we explain it? We don't know what it's all about." Monk looked helpless.

Chapter IV

THE FURNITURE POLISHER

The man had climbed out of a third-story window and slid down a drainpipe, thinking he was unobserved, and had crawled across a narrow strip of concrete driveway to the basement window of an adjacent house—this structure was an apartment building—which he had opened. He had vanished into the basement, walked through, and eventually found his way out the front door of the apartment house, as innocent as could be. He walked down the street, careful not to hurry.

Doc Savage spotted the man—he and Ham were idling across the street, at the edge of Central Park—as soon as the fellow appeared.

"You stay here," Doc told Ham. "See that Monk doesn't get in trouble with the police when he tries to explain this."

"I'll do what I can"—Ham sounded hopeful—"to see that the homely mug gets in jail."

Ham Brooks—his full name was Brigadier General Theodore Marley Brooks, and he was one of the country's leading lawyers, as well as a Doc Savage aid—conducted a kind of perpetual quarrel with the apish Monk Mayfair. He had never been known to make a civil remark to Monk, a favor which Monk had returned. Theirs was a strange sort of squabbling—each had risked his life to save the other on assorted previous occasions.

Doc Savage followed the man who had slipped out of the Radiator Smith mansion.

The fugitive was long and thin enough to be made out of fence rails, but he had a round face that was rather babylike, except that it was wrinkled. An elderly grapefruit would be a fitting article to compare to his head. His nose was negligible, although his mouth was ample and his eyes large and innocent. He wore a suit of coveralls, and carried under one arm a canvas bag that was somewhat shabby.

The fugitive crossed Fifth Avenue, entered Central Park, and quickened his pace enough to show that he had a definite destination. He hugged his canvas bag tighter.

The sky was darkening, for the sun had descended behind the thicket of skyscraper spires across the park to the west. It would soon be dark. The street lamps along the park driveways and sidewalks had already been turned on. The nurses and their baby carriages had disappeared for the day. There were a few bums with newspapers, looking for soft benches.

The man Doc was following traveled faster. He seemed to be walking about as fast as he could.

He stopped and bent over beside the walk, ostensibly to tie his shoe, but actually to pick up a rock and put it in the canvas bag.

Doc Savage got off the sidewalk and kept behind trees. Doc was not a conspicuous figure. He was still partially in disguise, of course—his hair was stained a black that contrasted greatly with its usual bronze hue, and his skin was also stained so that it was somewhat sallow instead of being a bronze that nearly matched his hair—so he was not recognized. Had he not been thus partially disguised, there was strong likelihood that some park loiterer would have recognized him. The bronze man was much better known than he would have liked to be.

Newspaper and magazine articles had publicized him as that strange and remarkable individual who made a business of righting wrongs and punishing evildoers who happened to be outside the law.

Doc continued to follow the lathy man with the worn canvas bag.

The fugitive came to one of the lagoons in Central Park.

He threw the bag as far out in the water as he could pitch it, when he thought no one was watching.

The man went on. Doc let him get out of sight, then waded out in the lagoon—it was not deep; the depth of most of the little lakes in Central Park is deceptive— and located the bag, got it and carried it ashore.

The bag contained the kind of stuff used by a furniture refinisher. Among the contents was a bottle of shellac and a bottle of alcohol.

The long, thin fugitive gave a nervous jump when Doc Savage appeared from behind a bush and stood suddenly in his path. Doc said, "Just a minute, if you don't mind."

The fugitive stared at the canvas bag—the one he'd thrown into the lake—which Doc was carrying.

"What's the idea?" he demanded uneasily.

Doc said, "A little over half the furniture in the room where Maurice Smith was found dead had been freshly polished with shellac and alcohol." Doc moved the canvas bag pointedly. "There is shellac and alcohol in here."

"Why, I . . . well—"

"Also," Doc added, "you climbed out of the Smith house through a third-story window and slid down a drainpipe."

The man swallowed. "It looks rather bad for me, I'm afraid."

"It sure does."

"I shouldn't have taken anybody's advice," the man muttered. "I should have stayed."

Doc said, "Suppose you tell a coherent story."

"My name is Oxalate Smith."

"Smith? Any kin to Radiator Smith?"

"No. The world is full of Smiths, you know."

"Yes. What were you doing in Radiator Smith's house?"

"I was hired to polish the furniture. I'm a furniture repairman and refinisher. I also have a small shop dealing in antique furniture. The butler—Jonas is his name—will tell you that he hired me."

"Why did you flee the house?"

Oxalate Smith twisted his hands together. His face was frightened.

"I was polishing the furniture in the library when Maurice Smith came in. I was a little over half done polishing, but Maurice Smith ordered that I leave the room, so naturally I did so. He told me I could come back and finish my polishing later. I went upstairs to work in one of the guest parlors."

"And then?"

"And then I heard that Maurice Smith had been murdered in the room where I had just been working."

"Murdered? Who told you it was a murder?"

"The girl—Annie Spain, she said her name was."

"Annie Spain?"

"She came to me upstairs. She said that Maurice Smith had been murdered, and they were accusing me. She said that they had found that potassium cyanide had been mixed with my furniture polish, and that it had killed Maurice Smith. She said they were going to have the police arrest me. She advised me to flee. I . . . well, I was terrified. I did as she suggested. I took my bag along, and threw it in the lagoon in the park, because I didn't want the police to find the potassium cyanide in my furniture polish."

Doc Savage shook his head slowly.

"You don't know much about potassium cyanide, do you?" he asked.

"I've always heard it was a deadly poison."

"It is. But you could hardly kill a man by putting it in polish then applying the polish to a piece of furniture which he used."

"Then I didn't—"

"Furthermore, Maurice Smith wasn't poisoned. He was killed by what apparently was a bolt of lightning."

"But—"

"You come back to the Radiator Smith house," Doc said. "If your story checks out, you will probably be turned loose."

The police had arrived at the Smith mansion and taken over. Monk, Ham and Long Tom were left with nothing to do. They met Doc Savage and Oxalate Smith on the sidewalk in front of the house.

"What do the police think?" Doc asked.

Monk said, "They don't know what to think. They're in there trying to figure out what killed Maurice Smith. We told 'em it was a lightning bolt, and they threw us out. They think we're crazy."

"Did you tell them why we are here?" Doc inquired.

"No. We don't know ourselves, do we?"

"Only that Radiator Smith got in touch with me by telephone, almost hysterical with fear, and wanted us to help him—and be very careful that no one knew we were helping him."

"I didn't tell the police anything."

Doc said thoughtfully, "I had better remove the rest of this disguise, or the police will get suspicious and take up our time asking us a lot of questions for which we haven't got answers. Where did you leave your car, Monk?"

"Two blocks south, just off Fifth."

Doc Savage walked to the car, a large sedan which was average-looking in size and color—only a close examination would show that the machine was armor-plated and had bullet-resistant glass—and climbed into the rear. Monk had returned his portable chemical laboratory to the machine. Doc mixed various chemicals and used the resulting paste to smear his hands, face and hair, after which the dye rubbed off readily.

The natural hue of his skin was a deep bronze, the product of exposure to tropical suns—the fact that his hair was a bronze color only slightly darker gave him a striking aspect.

He rejoined Monk, Ham, Long Tom and Oxalate Smith.

"Anyone found a trace of a girl named Annie Spain?" he asked.

Ham shook his head.

Oxalate Smith said nervously, "If the police find out about me fleeing, I'm afraid they'll throw me in jail on general principles."

"If we are convinced you are innocent," Doc said, "we will turn you loose."

"But can you—"

Monk told Oxalate Smith, "Doc Savage and the rest of us hold high honorary commissions on the police force. If we turn you loose, it'll be all right."

Doc suggested, "Monk, you go through Oxalate Smith's canvas bag of furniture-refinishing equipment and see if you find any potassium cyanide."

The big bronze man himself walked a block east of Fifth Avenue—this part of Fifth Avenue was a little too snazzy to permit the presence of anything so plebeian as a store—and found a corner cigar place with a telephone.

He looked in the telephone book. There was an *Oxalate Smith, Antiques, Repairing,* all right. It had a Second Avenue address. He called the number. A rather coarse voice answered.

"It is very important that I get hold of Oxalate Smith," Doc said.

"He ain't here," said the phone voice. "He's refinishin' some furniture at the home of Radi—of John R. Smith. You might get him there."

"Thank you," Doc said.

Monk reported, "No cyanide in that bag. No poison of any kind."

Oxalate Smith took a deep breath.

"The truth has just occurred to me, I think," he said. "That girl, Annie Spain, wanted me to flee that house and never come back and never tell anyone I had been there."

The dapper Ham said, "It looks that way."

"Annie Spain must be the killer," said Oxalate Smith

triumphantly. "She must have been afraid I could furnish incriminating evidence against her."

"Can you?"

"I think so," Oxalate Smith said grimly. "I saw her sneaking through the house, trying to let no one see her. I think she was following Maurice Smith."

"In that case, it looks bad for Annie Spain," Ham said.

Doc announced, "You may go."

"I'm free, you mean?" Oxalate Smith asked.

"Yes. You appear to be innocent."

"Gosh, thanks."

Chapter V

OXALATE SMITH AND THE FOOTPAD

It was very dark now. Oxalate Smith's round, wrinkled face was beaming in the street-light glow as he insisted on shaking hands with Doc and each of the others in turn, before taking his departure.

"I'm grateful to you. Everlastingly grateful," Oxalate Smith said. "If you want me, you know where my antique shop is. If I'm not there, I'll either be working or out in the country trying to buy some antiques cheap. Anything I can do for you, don't hesitate to call on me."

"That is nice of you," Monk said.

"You've done me a great favor. I would have been a fugitive from the law if it hadn't been for you. Good-by."

"Good-by."

Oxalate Smith walked away, heading in an easterly direction toward his shop. He walked slowly, holding his handkerchief in his hand and mopping his face. The relief of which he had just spoken was intense and genuine, and it was the nervous sweat that follows an intense strain that he was blotting off his features.

Madison Avenue and Park Avenue were brightly lighted—all of the north and south streets in this section were busy and brilliant ones—as he crossed them. He continued on crosstown. The cross streets were darker, and as he came nearer the East River, they took on a slum character.

The abrupt change from bright lights, rich apartments, regal homes, to a dismal slum section was typical of metropolitan New York, where rich men and beggar rub shoulders in the streets, and their homes do the same thing.

There were unpleasant odors, there was gloom, and the sidewalk was none too smooth.

The club came out of a darkened doorway. Maybe it was a fist. Oxalate Smith didn't see it, so he was not sure; later, when he examined his bruises on his jaw and found several marks that might have been made by knuckles, he suspected it was a fist.

Something came up and hit him very hard. It was the sidewalk.

A shadowy form—the individual who had put the slug on Oxalate Smith—unblended from the darkness of the doorway, and doubled over the unconscious man. Oxalate Smith was lifted. He was carried down the sidewalk a few yards to an unlighted car and dumped quickly inside.

The assailant stood by the car for a time, watching and listening, but there was no alarm. The assailant climbed into the back seat of the machine, where Oxalate Smith had been dumped.

In time—it must have been about half an hour later, he afterward concluded—Oxalate Smith regained his senses. A policeman was shaking him.

"Here, here," the policeman was saying. "You can't sleep on the sidewalk this way."

Oxalate Smith opened his mouth, then shut it. He clenched his teeth, trying to clear his head. The interior of his skull felt as if several blacksmiths were at work upon it. His stomach didn't feel so good, either.

"You sick, or something?" demanded the patrolman. "You was layin' here. Maybe I better call an ambulance."

Oxalate Smith got his wits organized.

"No," he said. "I don't need an ambulance."

"What ails you?"

Oxalate Smith made his voice thick and uncertain, like that of an intoxicated man.

"Jush one lil' drinky too mush," he said. "All of sudden, feel shleepy."

This was perfectly reasonable to the cop. He encountered drunks every night. His practice was to throw a scare into them so they would go home.

"I'm gonna call the wagon," the patrolman said, "and toss you in jail."

"No, no," said Oxalate Smith wildly. "Lemme go home."

The cop made a business of scowling and considering the point.

"Beat it," he said. "If I find you again, I'll run you in."

Oxalate Smith heaved to his feet and stumbled away. He was very glad to escape.

He'd had enough of the police this night.

"Ugh!" Oxalate Smith groaned, and held his stomach. His stomach felt terrible.

He rounded a corner, slowed up and explored in his pockets. The reason for the attack puzzled him. But it became clear when he discovered his pockets were empty. His billfold was gone, among other things.

"Some damned footpad," he complained. "As if I didn't have enough trouble!"

Chapter VI

THE TRAILING OF ANNIE SPAIN

Jonas, the butler, looked over the upturned end of his nose and said, "The master does not wish to see you, sir. He asks that you kindly leave the house, sir."

"He does, does he?" Doc said thoughtfully. "And why? He seemed very anxious to have us out here when he called on the telephone this morning."

"Begging your pardon, sir. But the master says he never sent for you. It must have been someone else."

Doc Savage walked past the butler, and the rather officious servant made a move to seize the bronze man, but Monk got in his way and exhibited a large hairy fist which had the properties—color and hardness—of a brickbat. "You just keep your shirt on," Monk advised. "We want to talk to this Radiator Smith."

The creator of the Smith radiator fortune was seated in one of the upstairs sunrooms. He looked up dully when they entered. He was pale; perspiration stood on his forehead as if he had a fever and it was breaking. The sinews were ridged out on his hands as they gripped the chair arm.

"You!" he said shrilly. "I told the police and the servants to keep you out of here."

Doc said, "You have recovered from your shock sufficiently to talk. We want to know why you called for us."

"I didn't," the wealthy man said flatly.

"You have a distinctive voice," Doc said quietly. "We made a recording of your telephone call, so we

31

can let you listen to your own voice if that would refresh your memory."

"It wouldn't—" Radiator Smith swallowed. "It must have been someone imitating my voice."

"What killed your son?"

The man tightened and breathed heavily for a moment. "I do not know."

"Why was he killed?"

The other shook his head dully.

Long Tom Roberts said, "I don't know whether you know it or not, but Doc Savage saved your life. You had an attack when your . . . when Maurice was killed. Doesn't that make any difference to you?"

Radiator Smith clamped his lips and said nothing.

Without pursuing the line of questioning further, Doc Savage turned and left the room. Homely Monk Mayfair overhauled the bronze man on the stairs.

"Doc, we could grab him and give him a shot of truth serum," Monk suggested.

"Later."

"Why not now?"

"His physical condition is still bad. He couldn't stand truth serum. The stuff is hard on the human system, you know."

In the central reception room downstairs, the big room just inside the main entrance, they found a number of police technicians gathered. Apparently they had finished their work at the Smith house.

Doc asked, "What was the verdict?"

"Killed by lightning," a man said gloomily. "Now it's up to someone to explain how lightning got into the room without leaving any marks, on a day when there wasn't any lightning."

There seemed to be nothing more that Doc Savage and his three aids could do. They were stymied. There was a perplexing mystery, but no clues, no leads they could follow.

"We might as well go get some sleep," Monk said glumly.

They walked to the sedan and climbed in. Doc

drove. The car was parked on a one-way street, and they waited at the junction with Fifth Avenue, at the corner nearest to Radiator Smith's great house, for the traffic light to change.

It was quite dark and clouds hid the stars. There was some traffic, not as much as usual. Across Fifth Avenue, on the wide sidewalk that paralleled Central Park, there was a peanut wagon presided over by a thin figure which was bundled in rags.

"Stop at that peanut cart," Monk suggested. "I want to get some peanuts for Habeas Corpus."

Habeas Corpus was Monk's pet pig.

Doc stopped the sedan beside the peanut wagon. An overhanging tree made the spot particularly gloomy, and the thin piping whistle of the peanut roaster was a ghostly sound.

While Monk was buying five sacks of peanuts, Doc made two rather strange remarks. He made them in a loud voice.

"Oxalate Smith certainly laid the crime on Annie Spain," he said. "If the police catch Annie Spain, they will probably electrocute her."

A moment later, he made the second remark.

"Oxalate Smith has been gone about an hour," he stated.

Monk got in the car with his peanuts, and Doc drove down the street.

"Doc, what did you mean by the talk about Oxalate Smith?" Ham asked in a puzzled voice.

Instead of answering, the bronze man took the first turn into a side street and yanked the sedan to a stop. He said, "Hand me a portable radio."

Long Tom passed a pocket radio outfit from the back seat. The apparatus was small, about the size of a folding camera, but it was capable of transmitting and receiving over very short wave lengths for distances up to fifty miles.

"Keep in touch with me," the bronze man said, and got out of the car.

"What's up?" Monk barked.

"That peanut vender," Doc said, "was Annie Spain."

There was astounded silence in the car as he left. Doc ran to the corner, slowed his pace to a more decorous one, and entered a cab. He rode in the cab past the peanut cart. The cart was in motion. The vender was wheeling it away from the spot where it had been standing—a spot where the Radiator Smith mansion could be watched to best advantage.

Well ahead of the peanut wagon, Doc alighted from the taxi, took to the park and loitered in its shadows, watching. His guess had been good. The vender wheeled the cart just far enough away that its being found abandoned in front of the Smith place would not seem suspicious.

The vender slipped into the park shadows. It was Annie Spain, all right. She slipped out of her ragged coat, stripped off the ancient trousers, got rid of a cap and bulky shoes. Under these garments she had been wearing her expensive tailored outfit. Her high-heeled slippers had been concealed somewhere around the cart. She put them on.

When she headed for the street, Doc ran, got there ahead of her and engaged a cab without being discovered.

The facilities of New York City's most densely populated section—this is Manhattan Island—for handling automobile traffic are generally conceded to exceed those of any other of the world's great metropolitan districts. The paramount artery for traffic in Manhattan is the elevated speedway running almost the entire length of the island on the west side, and leading northward to a system of scientifically designed parkways which enable the motorist to travel from Manhattan northward for a distance of more than fifty miles almost without pause and at a comparatively high rate of speed.

Annie Spain's taxicab followed the parkway well up into Westchester, the county of impressive suburban homes. The cab finally turned off, pulling into a drive-in restaurant.

The cab driver entered the restaurant. The place was equipped with a bar, and he began loafing there.

Annie Spain walked along a side road where darkness was almost complete. She used a tiny flashlight, the beam darting about nervously. Doc trailed her.

Doc used his little radio and told Monk and the others about the roadside restaurant and the cab driver idling in the bar.

"Find out what the girl told the driver to do," he instructed.

"Righto," Monk said. "Here's the restaurant now. I guess we weren't far behind you."

Annie Spain took a left turn. It was a winding road that mounted up an abrupt hill. Thick foliage banked each side of the road, then abruptly there was a stone wall and an arched gateway.

The young woman did not go near the gateway.

The gate was lighted brightly, and two men stood there, one holding a high-powered hunting rifle, the other an automatic shotgun.

Careful that the guards did not see her, Annie Spain reached the wall some two hundred feet from the gate, and cautiously climbed it.

Doc was close to her, and instead of waiting until she got over to climb the wall himself, did so while she was getting over, knowing there was less chance of the young woman hearing him at the moment.

Once across the wall, Annie Spain spent some moments in listening. During this interval, Monk's voice came over Doc's little radio, which he had tuned down until the speaker was hardly audible.

"The cab driver says the girl told him to wait," Monk explained. "Wait all night, if necessary. She gave him a ten-dollar bill and showed him a second one. She must be flush with money."

Doc whispered into the microphone, giving the location of the estate in which he now crouched. "Get up here," he said. "But do not show yourselves, and wait outside the gates."

"Seems like we're closin' in on somethin', huh?" Monk said.

The estate was as rich in a rural fashion as Radiator Smith's was palatial in the city. There was probably ten acres of yard. The house stood like a great dark block of stone on the top of a hill, dappled with white panels that were lighted windows. It was very late at night for so many windows to be lighted, particularly since there was no outward evidence of a party.

Annie Spain got close to the house and began examining the lighted windows. She went from one window to another, then appeared to locate one that was going to hold lasting interest for her, because she climbed a small tree.

Doc puzzled about the tree-climbing for a moment before he suspected the reason. Then he climbed a tree himself—his tree was farther back, but afforded almost as good a view of the lighted window as the other one. His guess proved correct. The grounds were patrolled.

Two watchmen passed. They had shotguns and flashlights, but went by without discovering either Doc or the girl.

The window was bulletproof, Doc saw. Light from within shone through in a manner that showed the glass had such thickness that it could only be bulletproof.

The room beyond was a comfortable study with a fireplace and pieces of furniture that were large. A desk occupied the central space. It was a vast piece.

The man who sat at the desk was likewise vast. Probably he could have lost a hundred pounds of weight and felt much better. His chins hung over his collar and his stomach pushed against the desk. When he put his hands down on the desk, they spread out like toy balloons filled with jelly.

The man was working—glancing over reports, signing papers, occasionally picking up the mouthpiece of a dictaphone to dictate. He used the telephone. He was smoking cigars, rich-looking cigars, each of which came in an individual glass container. The air in the room had a faintly bluish tinge because of the tobacco smoke.

After Doc had watched the fat man working for a while, he realized the fellow was scared. Terrified.

Also, he recognized the man. This man was named Smith, too. Doc had never met him. His name was J. Stillman Smith, and the newspapers called him Sell-'em-short Smith, because of his stock-market manipulations.

There was a rumor that Sell-'em-short Smith had made in excess of a hundred million dollars during various phases of the business depression, just by selling stocks and bonds short. The Federal government had once tried to indict him for something or other that had to do with raiding the stock market.

There were a lot of Smiths getting involved in the mystery, Doc reflected.

He was thinking about that when Sell-'em-short Smith began dying before his eyes.

Chapter VII

ANOTHER SMITH DEAD

Sell-'em-short Smith was talking over the telephone when the halo appeared around his head. The halo appeared suddenly—a strange phenomenon of luminous character, almost as bright as flame because it was plainly discernible in the lighted room. It was not flame. Rather, it was a weird bluish light that abruptly surrounded the fat man's head.

The fat man did not move for moments. He sat rigidly, gripping the telephone. His mouth was roundly open, and his eyeballs were slowly protruding more and more.

The aura of eerie bluish light around his head increased in volume, became a kind of fantastic corona of luminance, not bright enough to cast a light itself, yet very discernible in the brilliantly illuminated room.

There was a sound now. A low kind of a sound that might have been made by a locust, although of a somewhat faster beat than a locust note. It had started in a very muted degree, as if coming up out of inaudibility, but now it was louder, and there seemed to be many of the sounds; or possibly it was only the echo of the sound itself which made it seem many.

At no time did this sound ever become very loud. It was never as loud as a frog croaking, and hardly greater than a cricket's chirp. Probably it was the usual nature of the sound that made it so starkly noticeable.

Sell-'em-short Smith did not scream. But he did begin to rise up in his chair, every muscle in his body shaking.

Then a luminous thing that might have been his soul exuded from the top of his head. It came out slowly, like luminous vapor, and formed a kind of shapeless oblong blob and hung there in the air above the man's head, and still attached to his head.

Then the luminous thing gave a little hop and landed on the back of a nearby chair. It ran back and forth there, writhing, for an instant, then hopped up into the air of the room and hit the ceiling. It vanished there, as if it had gone through the ceiling.

The halo was gone from around Sell-'em-short Smith's head. The tightness was out of his body. He subsided loosely in his chair.

Doc Savage recovered from his astounded spell and realized Annie Spain was climbing down out of her tree. Being a woman wearing skirts, she was making it slowly.

Doc dropped out of his own tree, and stationed himself as a reception committee for the girl.

Because he did not want her screaming and attracting attention of the guards, he clamped a hand over her mouth.

"Quiet, you hear!" he warned.

She looked at him. There was enough reflected light from the window that she could discern his face. She made gestures indicating she wanted to speak. Doc lifted his hand.

"You're Doc Savage," she said.

"You know me, eh?"

"In my profession, naturally I would know you," Annie Spain said.

Inside the house, there was sudden excitement. A servant discovered the body and emitted a horrified bawling sound that was plainly audible. Instantly, people began running into the room where Sell-'em-short Smith sat loosely in the chair.

Doc said, "We better go back up the tree."

"We better run for it, you mean," Annie Spain said. "This place is alive with guards. After what's happened, they'll shoot, and ask questions afterward."

"The tree," Doc said.

They climbed a tree—both of them going up the same tree this time—and it was done none too quickly either, because two guards came racing past, driving long white flashlight beams into likely spots.

"My stockings!" Annie Spain complained. "They're a wreck. These trees!"

The stockings were a minor detail, considering the situation, Doc reflected. But he had noticed that women attached more importance to such things than they sometimes did to robberies and murders. He suspected he would never understand women.

He used the small radio. "Monk," he called.

"Yes," said the homely chemist's rather squeaky voice.

Doc reviewed the situation briefly. He finished, "You had better get up here and rescue us from this tree before they find us. Come in boldly. You have deputy State police commissions, so it should be all right."

"Right," Monk said. "If there's any fighting, save it until we get there."

Monk liked action.

Annie Spain was very silent for a moment. Then, "You were using a radio just now, weren't you?" she asked.

"Yes."

"I've heard a great deal about your scientific gadgets," the girl said. "I've wished I had some of them."

"What would you do with them."

"I would use them in my work."

The estate guards prowled under the tree again, so that it was not safe to continue the conversation. Down by the gate, there was a commotion. This uproar eventually subsided and Monk, Ham and Long Tom approached the tree.

Doc and Annie Spain climbed down out of the tree.

"Keep an eye on this girl," Doc suggested. "She seemed to know something was going to happen."

"I can explain everything," Annie Spain said.

"Smith is dead!" one of the guards blurted out.

"Yes," Doc Savage said. "It is a miracle if he isn't."

Monk demanded, "Did you see it, Doc?"

"Yes."

"What killed him?"

Doc Savage seemed not to hear the question. This was a small habit, this convenient loss of hearing, whenever he was asked something which he did not, for one reason or another—the reasons were usually good—care to answer.

Annie Spain eyed the bronze man.

"Go on. Tell them what it was," Annie Spain said. "Live up to your reputation."

Doc seemed not to hear that, either.

"I thought so!" said the young woman. "You don't know what killed him."

Doc ignored her.

"I always wondered if that whizz-bang reputation of yours wasn't a phony," Annie Spain said.

"Pipe down, sister," Long Tom ordered.

Annie Spain whirled on Long Tom. "Don't you tell me what to do, you mushroom-complexioned shrimp."

"Shut up, or I'll upset you," Long Tom said coolly. "I ain't very gallant."

They entered the house. In decorating the house, the owner had left no doubt that the place belonged to Sell-'em-short Smith. In every room there were pictures of Smith or trophies he had secured—mounted heads of big game, golf cups, framed honorary degrees. One room was papered entirely with clippings of newspaper stories concerning Smith.

Sell-'em-short Smith was dead.

Monk stared at the body. "Well, the lightning didn't kill this one—or did it?"

Doc Savage did not volunteer an explanation. He began examining the room.

Annie Spain stood around and looked baffled, and increasingly worried. They hadn't asked her a single question, and apparently she did not think that was natural.

The telephone over which Smith had been talking had fallen to the desk. Doc picked it up—or started to pick it up, rather. The instrument broke in his hands.

When it fell to the desk top, the telephone shattered into several dozen fragments.

"Hey!" Monk exploded, "that was a funny kind of telephone."

Doc did not touch the telephone again. He did poke at the cord. It fell to bits. It seemed brittle.

Long Tom said, "I'll be swiggered! There is no wire in that telephone cord."

Doc turned to one of the servants. "Is this telephone connected to any other instruments in the house?" he asked.

"No, sir," the servant explained. "It is a private telephone. The wire comes directly into the wall of this study from outdoors, I think."

"We can tell by an examination," Doc said.

"I don't think you can tell anything," Annie Spain asserted unpleasantly. "I think you're about nine-tenths fake."

Doc said, "Monk, take her out of the room—and watch her."

"With pleasure," Monk said.

Doc, Ham and Long Tom continued their investigation of the telephone line—and learned there was no line. No wire, at least. The insulators were on the poles, but there was no wire.

The bronze man moved along, poking a flashlight beam at the ground. Twice he picked up bits of shiny stuff.

"What's that you're finding?" Long Tom demanded.

Doc showed him.

"Metal that has been melted," Long Tom muttered. "You mean that something melted the telephone line?"

Doc did not explain what he meant.

The Sell-'em-short Smith servant force was in charge of a butler who was a fatherly, sensible fellow.

Doc asked him, "When did Smith begin acting scared?"

The butler said, "I noticed it a week ago. I mentioned it to him, sir. But he naturally denied it. He was a very blunt man, but a very secretive one, too."

"Did he scare easily?"

The butler pointed to the mounted head of a tiger on the wall. The tiger had been an enormous thing; the taxidermist had managed to capture a little of its ferocity.

"The master killed that tiger after it charged him and knocked him down," the butler explained. "He had climbed two of the highest mountains in the world in his time. As you know, sir, mountain climbing is not a pastime indulged in by—ah—pantywaists, if I may say so."

"You have no idea what scared him?"

The butler shook his head. "I know just one thing that might help."

"What is that?"

"I brought the master the newspapers tonight," the butler explained. "They contained a story about the death of another man named Smith—the son of Mr. John R. Smith, better known as Radiator Smith. The master read that story. He became very pale."

Doc asked, "Did the two Smiths know each other?"

"I do not think so. I have never heard it mentioned, if they did."

"Then there was no connection between the two Smiths that you know of?"

"No."

The dapper Ham said, "But there must be a connection somewhere."

"Maybe Annie Spain can explain it," Doc suggested.

They went to the room to which Monk had taken Annie Spain, a rather private room centrally located in the house, a room which had no windows, but depended on circulation from the air-conditioning shafts for its air.

Monk was standing outside the door with the makings of a spectacular black eye.

Chapter VIII

THE SERUM TRICK

"What happened to you?" Ham demanded.

"That girl," Monk said grimly, "hit me with an ash tray."

Ham grinned widely. Any minor misfortune to Monk always intrigued Ham.

"What were you trying?" Ham asked.

"Nothing," Monk growled. "We got to talking and I showed her some photographs of me I had in my pocket, and I just remarked that the pictures didn't do me justice."

"Then what?"

"She said I needed mercy, not justice, from a photographer."

"She was right. Then what?"

"I tried to reason with her. I told her fellows like me didn't grow on trees."

"And?"

"She said she guessed not. She'd never seen a tree with warts."

"I'm going to like that girl," Ham chortled.

"I asked her what was wrong with me," Monk said gloomily.

"Did she know?"

"She said nothing much, she guessed, although she thought they should have put my nose on my face bottom side up so that I would drown the first time it rained."

"I've often thought the same thing," Ham declared. "What happened then?"

"She just stood there and looked at me for a minute, then she up and hit me with the ash tray," Monk explained. "I don't understand it."

"If you would look in a mirror," Ham said, "you would not be so puzzled."

Doc pointed at the door. "She is still in there?"

"If she isn't, she's seven-eighths ghost," Monk said. "There are no windows in that room, and this is the only door."

They tried the door and it was locked. Doc knocked on the panel.

"Who is it?" Annie Spain called.

"Open up and stop this foolishness," Doc Savage said.

"Oh, it's you." The door opened immediately. "Your large monkey of a friend there seems to think he's a lady-killer," she said.

She stared at them, obviously wondering what they wanted. She looked remarkably chic, considering what she had been through. She had removed her stockings, which had gotten runs when she climbed the tree, but the fact that her legs were bare did not make the picture less interesting.

The room was comparatively bare, being fitted with two comfortable leather chairs, a table and a pair of reading lamps, which indicated it was a private study. In the corner was a washbasin with hot-and-cold-water faucets. Monk's portable chemical laboratory and a metal equipment case containing stuff they had thought themselves likely to need stood on the table.

"We are ready to ask you questions," Doc Savage told Annie Spain.

"It's about time," Annie said. "Get going on me."

"Monk," Doc said, "get the truth serum out of that equipment case."

Annie Spain gave a start and frowned unpleasantly. "Truth serum? Say, what is this?"

Doc said, "A long time ago, we discovered that it was practically impossible for us to tell when a woman was lying. They must have been equipped by nature as expert liars."

"I like that!" Annie Spain snapped.

"And so," Doc continued, "we give them truth serum whenever we can."

"Will the stuff hurt me?"

"It will be something like getting drunk, as far as the sensations are concerned. This is an advanced type of truth serum."

"Have I got any choice in this matter?"

"None."

"Let's get it over with, then."

Although Doc Savage's manner indicated that he put full trust in the truth serum, he was fully cognizant of the fact that the stuff had a degree of unreliability. There was nothing magical about it. The truth serum did not work legerdemain in the human mind and in some fashion separate lies from truth, so that only truth came forth; nothing as super-efficient as that. Rather, the serum simply dulled the mental processes to such an extent that the victim could not function enough gimp to think up a lie. The truth was conveniently at hand, so the dazed mind answered with the truth, unable to develop a falsehood.

The effects of the stuff, while not terribly unpleasant, were nevertheless a shock to the human system, and it was not a good idea to administer it to a person with a weak heart or lowered vitality.

Annie Spain took the stuff. After a while, her eyes became droopy and uncertain in their focusing.

"All right," Monk said. "We're ready to go."

Doc said, "Maybe you had better do the questioning, Monk. She is a little scared of you, hence more likely to answer your questions."

This was a psychological fact that the bronze man had discovered.

Monk got in front of Annie Spain. He said, "Who are you?"

"Annie Spain," said Annie Spain thickly.

"What are you?"

"I'm a young woman."

"What do you do?"

"The best I can."

Monk looked disgusted. Ham said, "You'll have to do better than that, Monk."

Monk made his voice louder and said, "Answer me! What were you doing in Radiator Smith's house?"

"I am a private detective," explained Annie Spain in a rather mushy voice. "I was trying to find out what was wrong with Radiator Smith."

"Was something wrong with him?"

"He was scared."

"How did you know that?"

"I eat in the same restaurant downtown where Radiator Smith eats lunch," Annie Spain said slowly, her eyes closed. "I saw that he was scared. I went over to him and told him what he needed was a good private detective. I asked him to hire me. He swore at me. I knew he was afraid. So I decided to help him anyway."

"Isn't that kind of unusual—helping him anyway?" Monk demanded. "What made you do it?"

"I needed a case. I haven't been making expenses with my detective agency."

"What did you learn?"

"That Radiator Smith was really scared. That a whole bunch of Smiths were in danger, and that the one most in danger, next to Radiator Smith, was Sell-'em-short Smith."

"How did you hear that?"

"Radiator Smith was talking over the telephone. I eavesdropped."

"Who was he talking to?"

"I don't know."

"Why did you flee from Radiator Smith's house?"

"The chauffeur got suspicious of me. I thought it was the regular chauffeur—it turned out to be Doc Savage."

"Why did you watch the house?"

"To learn anything I could."

"And why did you come up here to Sell-'em-short Smith's home?"

"To see what would happen. I wanted to solve this mystery and get famous—so I could make a lot of money in the private-detective business."

"Do you know what is behind this mystery?"

"No."

There were a lot more "No" answers before Monk gave it up.

"That's all she knows," Monk said. "She's a private detective who butted into the thing. Ain't that just like a woman?"

"We might as well leave her here," Doc Savage said, "until she comes out from under the effects of the stuff."

They left Annie Spain sitting in one of the deep chairs, departed from the room, closing the door and locking it behind them.

The young woman sat still for a time after Doc and his aids departed, then she cautiously opened one eye. The eye flicked about, making sure no one had remained in hiding in the room. Then she took in a deep breath, stood up and stretched and smiled widely.

She went to the washbasin in the corner and glanced down the drain. She turned the faucets, but no water came out. The faucets were not connected.

The fact that there was no water had discomfited her when she emptied the contents of the truth-serum phial into the basin earlier. But they had not noticed, fortunately, the presence of truth serum on the little screen in the drain.

Nor had they realized, Annie Spain decided triumphantly, that they hadn't given her a dose of truth serum at all. They had administered the dose she had rigged for them—a mixture of harmless chemicals she had quickly concocted from Monk's portable laboratory.

Annie Spain knew a great deal about chemistry.

But the deception had worked wonderfully. She had hit Monk in the eye with an ash tray as soon as she noticed the equipment case, and Monk had obligingly retreated from the room. Annie Spain had thought of the possibility of truth serum. That would explain why they had made no previous effort to question her.

She sank down in the chair and shook with silent glee.

"Doc Savage," she chuckled, "is easy to fool. He's greatly overrated."

A bit later, Doc Savage and the others returned to the room and inquired how she was feeling. Rather rocky, she admitted. She suggested that some fresh air might brace her, and Ham and Long Tom volunteered to accompany her.

Chapter IX

LONG TOM AND TROUBLE

Doc Savage remained in the room with Monk after the young woman left.

"I wonder what she did with the truth serum that was in the phial?" Doc Savage pondered.

"Huh?" Monk stared at the bronze man.

Doc Savage moved over to the washbasin and examined the drain closely. "This was the most likely place to get rid of it, at that," he remarked.

Doc went out to the car. He came back with three small jugs. They were black, made of composition, bakelite or something. About an inch and a half thick, three inches long, and not quite round, rather oval.

Doc gave one jug to Ham, another to Monk and another to Long Tom.

"What are these?" Monk asked.

"Part of an experiment we are trying," Doc explained. "Carry them with you. When you meet one of the crooks—if you do—get rid of the jug as soon as you can. Try not to let them see you. Put it where it can be found."

It was a little puzzling, but they did not ask questions. It was evidently some kind of an experiment.

"Long Tom," Doc said, "why don't you check on what has been picked up by the microphones you planted in Radiator Smith's home?"

"It will be a waste of time, if you ask me," Long Tom suggested. "When Radiator Smith first called on us for help, we decided to plant the mikes as a matter of taking our usual precaution to check every angle of anything we go up against.

"We know the microphones didn't pick up anything before Maurice Smith was murdered."

"They might have since."

It required a full hour for Long Tom Roberts to drive back to Manhattan Island, and another half hour for him to collect the recordings picked up by the microphones he had planted in the Radiator Smith mansion on Fifth Avenue. He had installed his recording devices in an empty apartment in a swanky apartment house adjacent to the Smith manse.

Playing back the recordings occupied more time. Long Tom used a system—he raced the recordings through until the playback encountered a voice, when he slowed up and listened. The recordings were impressed magnetically upon a long wire.

He got nothing until he came to the recording made by a microphone he had planted close to the rear door. He'd placed a mike there because he happened to recall that important things are often said, or repeated, when persons stand at a door in arriving or departing.

The interesting recording went:

Voice: (A voice Long Tom had never heard before.) *Hello. I want to see Jonas. The butler.*

Maid: (Long Tom recalled this voice as a Smith maid.) *Wait here. I'll try to find him.*

A long interval of silence.

Jonas: *Yes . . . Great grief! Who told you to come here? It's too dangerous—*

Voice: *They want you downtown.*

Jonas: *Me?*

Voice: *You and everybody else. There's a get-together.*

Jonas: *But why? What's gone wrong?*

Voice: *Plenty, I guess. A guy named Doc Savage is messing around in it now, and that means we've got to be careful. I think this meeting is a kind of roundup to straighten everybody out on their duty and give them a line on what happens next. And what they're to do to help.*

Jonas: *When is the meeting?*

Voice: *About two o'clock in the morning. Just when the night clubs are letting out.*

Jonas: *Well . . . I can make it. I'll leave here about one-thirty. Fortunately, the police have not left anyone on guard.*

Voice: *Be seeing you then, huh?*

Jonas: *Yes. I'll be there.*

That was the end of that, and it was quite enough. Long Tom snapped off the playback, yanked back his cuff and stared at his wrist watch. A quarter after one.

"Blazes, I gotta make it!" Long Tom blurted. He snatched up an eavesdropping device and charged for the nearest taxi stand.

Long Tom had taken the recordings to Doc Savage's downtown headquarters—the playback apparatus was there—and hence he was some distance from the elegant part of Fifth Avenue where stood the Radiator Smith home. But he made it with probably three minutes to spare.

The office building stood on Broadway, in the theatrical district, in the middle of a glare of electric lights that was almost daytime bright. The place had two disadvantages—noise and twenty-four-hour-a-day activity—but out of these might spring an advantage. Men could enter or leave the place at any time during the twenty-four hours with small chance of attracting attention from, for instance, the police.

Long Tom Roberts watched the butler, Jonas, enter the building.

Long Tom looked rather like a Broadway tout. He had a fish-belly complexion, as if he was never abroad in the daytime, and there were plenty of those on the street around him. No one gave him a second glance. He walked into the building behind Jonas.

It occurred to Long Tom that he had neglected to inform Doc Savage what he was doing, but there had really been no time for that.

Jonas took an elevator. There was an indicator over the elevator door, and it moved around to nine, indicating the cage had gone to that floor. It made only the one stop—this was an out-and-out break of luck—which indicated that Jonas had been the only passenger.

Long Tom wrote a note on a piece of paper and dropped it in a mailbox.

Then Long Tom took to the stairs. He didn't know but what the elevator operator might be in cahoots with Jonas and the others.

The ninth-floor hallway proved to be full of doors. It offered a problem. Long Tom waited in the stair well. There was to be quite a gathering here, he'd understood from the recording. He hoped Jonas wasn't to be the last one to arrive—

Several minutes later a ratty-looking fellow— "crook" was written all over him—scurried out of the elevator and hurried to a door. He knocked several times, unevenly, in a signal, then disappeared inside.

Long Tom spotted the door, and as soon as it was closed he glided down the corridor. His objective was either one of the doors to the right or left of the one through which the man had disappeared. He reached one of them. It was locked, but the lock was simple, and Long Tom knew something about picking locks. He got the door unfastened.

He opened the door very carefully until he was sure there was darkness inside, then stepped in quickly. The place smelled very faintly of disuse.

It was utterly dark. The complete blackness puzzled Long Tom, for Broadway outside was so bright, and if there was a window—but there wasn't any window. That was it. The whole side of this building was walled up to afford a background for one of the Great White Way's fabulous electric signs. That explained the windowless office.

A crack of light came from under the door to the adjacent office. So there was a door! Growing more elated by the moment, Long Tom tried the door very cautiously—he didn't want them walking in on him—and found it locked.

He attached his eavesdropping device. It consisted of a pick-up microphone which was held against the door panel by adhesive strips, the panel serving as a sounding board. There was a small amplifier, a headset and plenty of cord.

Having planted the pick-up, Long Tom struck a match and gave the office a brief examination. There was a yellow oak desk with a desk lamp, some hard chairs, and an elderly rug.

On the desk stood an ordinary crystal microphone on a stand.

Long Tom was ogling the microphone in astonishment when a key clicked in the door lock.

Long Tom had not become an electrical wizard without learning to think. He made a dive, reached the spot where the cord from the desk lamp plugged into a wall outlet. He pulled the outlet plug out a trifle, whipped a silver half-dollar from his pocket and jammed it against the brass lugs, short-circuiting them. There was a spit of blue flame; somewhere else the faint pop of a fuse blowing.

They wouldn't be able to turn on the lights in here now and discover him.

A moment later, he began to doubt that the lights would have been turned on anyway.

The figure which entered the room—it was outlined briefly against the hall light—was swathed in an enormous tan topcoat of the wrap-around variety. The topcoat collar was turned up; a large hat was yanked down low. The door clicked shut the instant the newcomer was inside.

Astonished, Long Tom realized he not only hadn't recognized the visitor—he didn't even know whether it was man or woman.

He listened in growing amazement.

The visitor lost no time in taking a seat at the desk and beginning to speak into the microphone. First, there was a faint clicking sound. Long Tom knew what that meant when the other began talking. Some kind of gadget—probably a short tin tube—placed between the lips to disguise the whispering.

Whispering! The visitor spoke entirely in a whisper, and it was shrill and unnatural, yet quite understandable. But whether it was a man or woman talking, it was impossible to tell.

"Are all of you present?" the whisperer asked. "Jonas will you answer? Speak in a loud voice so that you may be heard."

From the other room, Jonas answered, "Everybody here."

Long Tom knew that the whispering was being stepped up by a battery amplifier and put out through a loud-speaker in the adjacent room.

"I have called you here in order to give you certain commands and thus tighten our organization," said the whisper. "As you know, one Smith died this afternoon. Another has also died, as your morning newspapers will reveal. The other Smiths will die as scheduled, and thus everything will continue according to plan. Do not worry about that."

There was a pause. In the adjacent room, the whisper from the loud-speaker must be an eerie thing, and the author of the sound probably knew it. The pause was to let it take full effect.

"More Smiths will die," the whisper continued. "But there are others we will have to include with the Smiths. A man named Doc Savage and his associates."

Long Tom was an impulsive fellow. He decided he'd heard enough. He had the master mind of the gang here in the room with him, so what was the use of fooling around any longer?

Long Tom came up out of the corner where he had been crouching, fished in an underarm holster and brought out an unusual weapon called a supermachine pistol, a gun which Doc Savage had developed. The weapon was capable of firing hundreds of shots a minute; it could put bullets out a great deal faster than a man could feed them into the mechanism with clip magazines, in fact.

Long Tom remembered the jug—the little black thing that Doc had given him. He was supposed to get rid of that as soon as he contacted the culprits. He pulled it out of his pocket. There was a wastebasket close, and he shoved the jug into that.

Then Long Tom started for the figure at the desk— and forgot all about the lamp cord on the floor. His toe hooked it. He practically stood on his head.

His finger tightened on the machine-pistol trigger and it roared like a big bullfiddle.

"Help!" rasped the whispering voice. "The next room to you! South! Help!"

Long Tom fumbled on the floor. He had lost the pistol; the recoil of the thing had made it jump out of his hand.

Before he found the gun, a flashlight beam jumped at him from the desk. The moment the light impaled him, Long Tom surged up and charged. He dived over the desk, hit a figure. They crashed to the floor. The flashlight flew to one side, glanced off the wall and landed so that its beam was pointed partially at their figures, enough that there was light for Long Tom to identify his foe.

"You," Long Tom exploded. "Damned if I'd ever have guessed *you* were the killer!"

There was no more conversation, and not much more action, because Jonas ran in and crashed a chair down on Long Tom's head.

Chapter X

DEATH FOR SMITHS

It was about this time that Doc Savage and Monk Mayfair heard a racket outside Sell-'em-short Smith's house in Westchester. The noise—it was a frenzied pounding—came from the garage; or rather from a room over the garage.

They unlocked the door.

Ham stumbled out. Ham had a skinned place on the side of his head, and a desperate expression.

"Why, shyster, I thought you were supposed to be watching Annie Spain," Monk said. "You took over that job when Long Tom left."

"She hit me with a wrench. Then she locked me in that upstairs garage room, I guess. Anyhow, I was there when I came to my senses."

"Where did she go?"

"If she isn't around, it's obvious. She skipped."

"When did this happen?"

"A good two hours ago. Not very long after Long Tom left."

It was almost dawn when they returned to Doc Savage's headquarters.

The headquarters occupied the eighty-sixth floor of one of the town's most impressive skyscrapers, and consisted of three general divisions—a reception room, a library, and a laboratory where the bronze man conducted his endless scientific experiments.

They were trying to get some sleep, and keeping each other awake by talking—when Annie Spain turned up. Monk opened the door.

57

"Annie Spain!" Monk exploded. "Blazes!"

The young woman entered the place rather sheepishly.

"I'm sorry I skipped out," she said. "I wanted to continue this investigation by myself."

"Why?"

"Because I wanted to hog the credit." Annie Spain looked uncomfortable. "But I thought it over. This is a little too big for me. Maybe a little too mysterious. I want to work with you fellows."

Monk felt of his eye. "So far, you've only worked *on* us," he ventured.

"I'll be nicer," Annie Spain promised.

They ran the recordings which Long Tom had made of the microphone pick-ups at the Radiator Smith home, and discovered the incriminating evidence against Jonas, the butler. They rushed up there.

But Jonas was not there, and he did not come back.

During the next day it dawned on Doc Savage with unpleasant force that a widespread campaign against people named Smith was in progress.

The earliest editions of the morning newspapers carried the story of the death of Sell-'em-short Smith and a rehash of the earlier stories about the demise of Maurice Smith, son of Radiator Smith.

But the noon edition came out with the story of the death of Telegraph Smith, who was also known as Michael Robertson Smith, III, of very aristocratic lineage, heir to a telephone and telegraph-company fortune.

Telegraph Smith had been driving down to his office when lightning struck his town car. It was a perfectly clear day, and no clouds, but as near as anyone could tell, lightning struck the car.

"Very similar to the death of Maurice Smith," Doc said grimly.

The bronze man and his two aids, Monk and Ham—they were beginning to wonder what had happened to Long Tom—reached the death scene, but the town car and the body had been removed.

From Telegraph Smith's secretary they got a bit of information that was interesting.

"Mr. Smith," said the secretary, "told me someone had threatened his life several days ago."

"Who?" Doc asked.

The secretary didn't know.

Doc made extensive inquiries, but he learned nothing more of real value until he heard of the death of Shipowner Smith.

Shipowner Smith was plain Henry Smith, but there was nothing plain about the fortune he had amassed in the transatlantic passenger business.

He died while watering his flowers. He was using a hose for the sprinkling. No one saw it happen.

Doc picked up the hose. It broke in his hands. He could crush it in his fingers. The rubber and fabric of the hose, it was obvious, had undergone some kind of strange change.

The vice president of Shipowner Smith's corporation gave them some information.

"Smith told us," said the vice president, "that he had been ordered to turn over control of his business interests to some person. He was to remain the head of them, but he was to take orders from this person, and give this person a share of the profits. He was threatened with death if he did not comply."

"When was that?" Doc asked.

"Four days ago."

"Did he know who threatened him?"

"No."

Doc Savage and his two aids, Monk and Ham, investigated thoroughly, without unearthing anything that seemed to mean much. At least, what they found meant nothing except more bafflement to Monk and Ham.

Annie Spain was with them, and she said disgustedly that it didn't mean anything to her, either.

"What became of Long Tom?" Annie demanded. "Not only you haven't learned anything, but you've lost one of your men, if anybody asks me."

"You're sure a quarrelsome person," Monk told her.

Doc paid Radiator Smith a visit.

Because the bronze man knew he was as much inside the doghouse as he could get as far as Radiator Smith was concerned, Doc stalked past a phalanx of secretaries and into the great man's presence without being announced.

Radiator Smith sprang up with a gasp and quickly shoved a bundle of papers into his desk.

Doc wasted no time on politeness. He strode to the desk, pulled the drawer open and took the papers out. Radiator Smith pawed futilely at him, trying to prevent him seeing the documents.

The papers were headed:

OPERATING ORDERS

Doc ran his eyes over them. They were simply typed directions telling Radiator Smith how to run his many enterprises. There was no clue as to who had written them, but it certainly had not been Radiator Smith.

"Give me those!" Radiator Smith gasped.

Doc returned the documents. The man was pallid, perspiring and shaky.

"This explains your behavior, doesn't it?" Doc remarked.

Radiator Smith sank weakly in his chair.

"Like the other Smiths, you were ordered to turn over management of your interests to someone, or be killed," Doc said. "In your case you were told your son would be killed."

Radiator Smith made an inarticulate noise. His hands were knotting.

"You ignored the threat and summoned us," Doc said. "Your son, Maurice, was immediately killed. That changed your mind.

"I do not believe I blame you. But can you give us any information that will help us?"

Radiator Smith shook his head slowly.

"I couldn't," he said, "if I wanted to."

Chapter XI

THE HEIR

The note from Long Tom Roberts arrived late that afternoon. It had been delayed because it was not even in an envelope; it was merely a sheet of paper, and there was postage due, for there had been no stamp on it in the first place.

It was the note Long Tom had written in the lobby of the building on Broadway.

It simply stated that Long Tom had followed Jonas to the ninth floor of the building.

Twenty minutes later, Doc Savage and the others were standing in the building. Another five minutes were expended in locating the room where Long Tom had met his bad luck.

There were fight signs about. The desk was upset, and one chair had been broken. The microphone, its amplifier, and the loud-speaker in the next room were all in place. So was Long Tom's listening gadget. The stuff told an understandable story.

"Long Tom got in here to eavesdrop," Doc said thoughtfully. "He was probably surprised by someone who came to talk, using that loudspeaker, to someone in the next room."

Monk picked up a piece of tin. It was like a flattened tube, about two inches long.

"What's this?" the chemist pondered.

Annie Spain said, "Probably used to disguise a voice. I have a hunch that if one spoke through that, and whispered, too, that the voice would be unrecognizable."

Monk grinned. "That's such a good guess," he said, "that I almost suspect you of being here."

Ham twirled his cane—the innocent dark cane contained a sword, and he never went without it—and looked thoughtful. He said, "The big point is: Any sign of who did the talking through the loud-speaker—the headman?"

"It couldn't have been the butler, Jonas, at any rate," Monk said.

"What makes you think so?" Ham demanded.

"Long Tom followed Jonas here, didn't he? He wouldn't have come into this room with Jonas here and had time to attach his listening-in device to that door."

"Jonas could have come from the other room to this one."

Doc Savage examined the wastebasket. He found Long Tom's jug, the small black thing, the shell of which was made of bakelite. The bronze man went to the window, stood looking at the device.

The others did not notice that he had found the little contraption. He did not tell them.

The bronze man's face was sober, his manner concerned as he moved slowly about the room. Then abruptly—as though there was something important suddenly in his mind demanding immediate action—he left the building. Monk and Ham remained behind.

They found nothing of value, but did discover that fingerprints had been wiped off anything that might have retained them. The rooms had been rented by mail, they discovered, and no one around the building had ever seen the individual who had taken them.

"Doc knew those guys would be too slick to leave any clues," Monk said. "That's why Doc left. Wonder where he went?"

Doc Savage turned up shortly in the city room of one of the town's most blatant tabloid newspapers. His entrance created quite a commotion, because the bronze man was distinctly the stuff of which newspaper headlines are made, as well as being handsome enough to make excellent camera fodder.

Doc Savage assumed a forbidding manner. "I have come here to tell you," he announced, "that you had better stop publishing matter concerning myself and my associates. In particular, you must not publish anything concerning Long Tom Roberts."

The city editor wasn't the city editor of that hell-raising tabloid because he could be bluffed. Several times in his hectic career, he had told senators, and even the president, where they could go, as far as he was concerned.

"Yeah!" he said. "Oh, yeah? Let me tell *you* something. This rag publishes news, and anything that happens is news, and if you don't like that, see our lawyers!"

"You refuse to co-operate?" Doc asked.

"Co-operate? You're a fine one to talk about co-operating!" The city editor turned purple. "How many times have you thrown my reporters out? How many times have you refused to give interviews?"

It was quite a few times, but Doc skipped the point.

"I see there is no use talking to you," the bronze man said.

Doc turned away. He deliberately acted nervous, and drew out his handkerchief to mop his forehead.

A yellow envelope came out with Doc's handkerchief and fell to the floor, the bronze man apparently not noticing. He walked away.

The city editor had seen the envelope fall, but he sat there without saying anything. As soon as Doc had gone, he snatched up the envelope.

It was a cablegram envelope. The city editor opened it and read the contents.

"Jumping cats!" he said. "Joe!" he yelled. "Hold page two." The city editor slammed the cablegram down on his desk and grabbed a typewriter. "Try to keep me from publishing news about his friends, will he!" he growled. "I'll show him!"

The first editions of one of the morning papers—the editions which hit the streets about eight o'clock—carried a story that astounded Doc Savage's associates. Monk was gazing idly at the loudest tabloid of them all when his eyes popped.

"Great grannies!" he yelled.

"What's wrong?" Ham demanded.

"Look!" Monk exploded. "Just look at this!"

Ham leaned over Monk's shoulder and read the story which had astounded the homely chemist to such a degree.

"By jove!" Ham said thoughtfully. "And here we've been treating him like he was a common working guy like the rest of us."

The story:

ELECTRICAL
WIZARD INHERITS FORTUNE

Major Thomas J. Long Tom Roberts
Heir to South Africa Gem
Millions

It was learned today that Major Thomas J. Long Tom Roberts, New York electrical engineer, has inherited an estate of at least ten million dollars from his uncle, Cunico Roberts, of Cape Town, South Africa. Cunico Roberts is reported to control one of the greatest diamond fortunes in existence.

In addition to the cash, it is understood Long Tom Roberts will inherit extensive holdings in diamond-mine properties.

Ham finished reading and said, "That amazes me! I never heard Long Tom mention a rich Uncle Cunico."

He and Monk rushed with the tabloid newspaper into the laboratory, where they found Doc Savage.

"Doc!" Monk exploded. "What does this mean?"

The bronze man took the tabloid and studied the story with approval.

"Contains almost exactly what was in the cablegram," Doc remarked.

"I don't understand this," Monk was puzzled.

"It simply means," Doc explained, "that a particularly obnoxious city editor swallowed a bait."

Chapter XII

THE LIFE PRESERVER

Long Tom Roberts fully understood that he was alive only because it was more convenient to take a live man from place to place than it was to transport a dead one.

They were going to kill him. They had told him so, and he believed them. This was merely an interval of delay.

There might have been another reason for his not being killed immediately—they could have been keeping him alive in order to get information from him, to find out how much Doc Savage actually knew, and how close upon their trail the bronze man was running. But Long Tom thought not. The leader of this gang was remarkably well posted, and unafraid.

They had been questioning Long Tom, beating him in a desultory fashion while they did so, but he believed they were merely marking time in that fashion. His real objective was death, and the delay only one of convenience.

At the end of the present trip, he would die, probably. So he was not anxious to see it terminate. He sat back in the big, ancient touring car, and while he was not happy, at least this was better than what he had to look forward to.

They were in southern Maine somewhere. They had passed through much nice scenery, which Long Tom was in no mood to enjoy, and they were following back roads now, as they had followed them throughout the trip. It had been slow driving, and Long Tom had not dreamed there was such a remote and unpopulated route through Connecticut and Massachusetts.

There were four men in the machine, and they were not at all sociable. For crooks, they were remarkably loyal fellows. Not a word had been spoken about their boss, and Long Tom had two teeth that felt loose because he had tried to insist on talking about the master mind.

The master mind had been piqued over the necessity of revealing identity; mad as the devil, in fact. But there had been no alternative under the circumstances, so the leader had made the best of it, even seeming somewhat pleased at the astonishment which was manifest on some faces when it was discovered just who the master mind was.

Two men rode beside Long Tom, one at either elbow, and he was handcuffed to them. They had cheap, phony deputy-sheriff stars which they had pinned on their vests, and the two men in the front seat also had phony stars; this was a ruse in case they should be stopped by anyone.

Where they were bound, Long Tom was not sure. But he did know that they planned to shoot him to death when they reached a particularly remote stretch of road close to the coast, and toss his body over a cliff with a rock tied to it so that it would sink in deep water.

Suddenly, without the slightest warning, an automobile careened past them, skidded to a stop directly ahead.

One of the men cursed, and drew a pistol.

"Wait, it's Lopez," his companion said.

Lopez was a long, pale man, and he came galloping up in a lather of excitement.

"You ain't killed him yet?" he barked. Then he observed the evident fact that Long Tom was alive. "Gee, I caught you in time!"

"What's eating you?"

"Chief's orders not to kill this guy under any circumstances," said Lopez.

"Huh! Why?"

"It seems he's inherited ten million dollars and some diamond mines."

Long Tom sat back, no little surprised, but with the wits to hold his tongue and look wise. So he had inherited ten million dollars, had he? He hoped it was true.

He was aware of a new attitude of respect toward him on the part of his captors. They were even solicitous about his comfort. A few moments ago he had been no more to them than a hog they were taking to the butchering pen, but now they had a personal interest in him.

"Ten million dollars, eh?" Long Tom remarked. "And some diamond mines. Well, well!"

"Did you know your Uncle Cunico well?" Lopez asked.

"Who—"

"Uncle Cunico, the man who left you the dough."

"Oh, you mean Uncle Wilbur—I guess maybe they called him Cunico," Long Tom said. "Yeah. A great guy, Uncle Wilbur."

He was being cagy, taking no chances that they might be feeding him the name of a fake relative in order to trap him. He had no Uncle Cunico. He had no Uncle Wilbur, for that matter.

"My handcuffs hurt me like hell," he said. "How about taking them off my wrists and putting them on my ankles?"

"I don't know," one of the captors said doubtfully.

"I'll give you a check for fifty dollars," Long Tom said.

That did the trick, and Long Tom's first act after having his wrists freed was to write a check. They had left him his fountain pen, but he had some difficulty making it write, scratching around on the check for a while without making visible marks, and finally borrowing a pen from one of the men. He made out the check and signed it, and they rolled northward in harmony.

"Where are we going?" Long Tom asked innocently.

They grinned at him; he had asked the question before, and gotten no satisfaction. The only difference was that this time they grinned at him, instead of slugging him in the face.

He sat back and pondered the question of the ten million and the diamond mines. It made nice pondering. But he did not let delight carry him away. He smelled a trick.

It was a fact that whoever had created the illusion that he had inherited ten million dollars had saved his life.

"Doc Savage," Long Tom remarked after a while.

The captors stared and one demanded, "What?"

"I was just thinking," Long Tom said. "What do you reckon Doc thinks became of me?"

Lopez—he was riding in the car now—answered that question.

"Doc Savage is going to think you are in South America," said Lopez.

"How come?"

"You're going to write a cable."

"I'm not in South America."

"That's all right. You write the cable, and we'll send it down there and a friend of ours will cable it back."

"I don't need to write it," Long Tom said. "A cable doesn't come in the handwriting of the man who sent it. It comes off one of those simplex machines in typing."

Lopez looked sheepish. "That's right," he said. "I'll just write the cable out myself, and we'll send it soon."

Chapter XIII

TRAIL TO MAINE

It was a very convincing cablegram which Lopez had composed and which landed in Doc Savage's hands several hours later after having gone the roundabout route to South America:

It read:

ESCAPED FROM GANG AND GOT HOT TIP AND AM TRAILING HEAD CROOK IN PERSON STOP HAVE REACHED MARACAIBO VENEZUELA BY PLANE AND FOLLOWING MASTER MIND INLAND STOP THINK CENTER OF WHOLE MYSTERY IS DOWN HERE IF YOU CAN COME DO SO IN HURRY

LONG TOM

"It's a fake," Doc Savage said.

Monk nodded soberly. So did Ham. "It's a phony," they agreed.

That would have puzzled Lopez. And puzzled Annie Spain. She read the cablegram, then called the cable office and learned the missive really had come from Maracaibo, Venezuela.

"Listen, how do you know the message isn't genuine?" she demanded.

Ham grinned. "Hunch," he said.

"Hunch, eh? You're crazy," Annie Spain said with no approval.

Annie Spain got on the telephone and canvassed the air lines which operated planes southward, and particularly to South America.

"Come here and listen to this," she told Doc Savage.

The voice from the airline office said, "Yes, our records show that a man named Long Tom Roberts left on one of our planes yesterday. He had a ticket to South America."

"When would he have reached Maracaibo?"

"Today."

"Can you describe the man?"

"Why, I'll have to see if someone remembers him, and call you back. Is it important?"

"It's darned important," Annie Spain said.

While they were waiting for the airline office to call back, Doc Savage said, "You are a rather persistent young woman, aren't you, Miss Spain?"

"I'm trying to be a good detective," Annie Spain said. "I notice."

"A good detective doesn't pass up any bets—and doesn't play hunches."

"You are fully as anxious as we are to get a trace of the villains, I've noticed."

"Well, why not?"

"I don't know why not," Doc Savage said. "The point just struck me, is all."

The telephone rang. It was the airline office. He said that a field porter and the driver of the bus which the line operated at the airport both remembered Long Tom Roberts. They gave a description of an under-sized, mushroom-colored fellow who sounded very like Long Tom.

"You see!" Annie Spain ejaculated triumphantly. "Your hunch is wrong!"

"It's an awful strong hunch," the dapper Ham told her.

"You mean you're not going to do anything about this cablegram saying Long Tom is in South America, and asking you to hurry down there?"

"Nothing."

"Oh, you fools!" exclaimed Annie Spain.

The complex system of living which modern man has evolved and which he calls civilization has many wonders besides airplanes and radios, and some of these are not as well known as they should be. Clearing houses, for instance—the clearing houses through which banks clear the checks given to them upon other banks. These work as fast as the mails will allow, and sometimes faster. A check given on a New York bank and cashed in Maine, for example, takes surprisingly little time to reach the New York banks, thanks to the facile clearing-house system.

Doc Savage answered the telephone.

"Yes," he said. His speech was confined almost entirely to affirmative. "Yes," he said again. Then, "Yes. Send it up immediately."

Twenty minutes afterward, a bank messenger arrived with a canceled check. It was for fifty dollars.

"What's that?" Annie Spain wanted to know.

"Just a nibble on a line we had out," Doc said, which did not explain anything.

It was Long Tom's check, the one he had given to his captor.

Doc put it under ultraviolet light. This ultraviolet, or "black" light, as it was called, has the peculiar property of causing some substances to flow, or fluoresce.

Long Tom's fountain pen, instead of being empty, had been filled with an ink which was ordinarily invisible, but which glowed when exposed to black light. There was a message on the check that had nothing to do with the visible writing on it.

Going north on Woodhill Road from Turpin Corners Maine blue sedan NYOO-319

Doc Savage—he had used the black light in the laboratory—went quickly into the reception room.

"The plane," he said. "We are leaving immediately."

Annie Spain sprang up. "So you're finally going to South America!" she ejaculated.

"Of course."

"Do you want to go along?" Doc asked.

"Fine. We would have taken you anyway."

Annie Spain stared at the bronze man. She hadn't liked his remark. "Just what did you mean by that crack?" she demanded.

Doc said nothing.

The bronze man kept his planes in a huge brick combination warehouse and boat hangar on the Hudson River waterfront. The structure masqueraded as a warehouse, and was reached by an underground tube of an affair through which a bullet-shaped car traveled, a contraption that Monk called the "angel wagon," or the "go-devil" depending on the mood he was in.

Doc loaded a motorcycle aboard the plane.

They took off in a dual-motored, single-wing monoplane which looked like a pursuit bomber, and could outfly most of them. It was slightly unusual as to structure—although this did not spoil its streamlining—in that it could land on earth or water. For water service, the landing gear was merely cranked up, disappearing into the hull.

Doc set a course.

"Say," Annie Spain yelled, "you are not heading toward South America!"

"Not on your life. That was just your idea."

"You mean that you still don't intend to do anything about that cablegram?"

"The cable was a fake."

"How do you know? It checked out genuine. Long Tom took the plane. The cable was really sent from South America."

Doc explained, "Our enemies aren't fools. They had a man who resembled Long Tom take the plane south. We will radio the South American police to have that fellow arrested, incidentally. Any friend of the crooks could have relayed the cable."

"But what makes you so sure?"

"There is a password," Doc said, "which all of us invariably include in any message sent to each other, if that message is genuine."

Annie Spain sat back. She looked rather floored.

Turpin Corners was not on most atlas maps of the State of Maine, and a few road maps had missed it. There was a grocery store, filling station, post office, dance hall, all in one building that would probably fall down in another three or four years.

Woodhill Road was the only road through Turpin Corners, and it extended northward, more crooked than it seemed possible for a road to be, and unpaved.

Ten miles north of Turpin Corners, Doc Savage set the plane down and unloaded the motorcycle. He explained to the others.

"You fellows keep on and look for blue sedans," he said. "Get that license number into the hands of the State police, and have them broadcast it to every county sheriff and town constable."

"You'll look from the road?" Monk inquired of his chief.

"I'll look from the road," Doc agreed.

The plane climbed into the air again. Doc got on the motorcycle and headed up the road, pulling a long worm of dust after him. The road was rough. There were a few farms, but most of the time nothing but hills coated with scrubby trees. During the next fifteen minutes, Doc passed no traffic whatever.

Coming to a filling station, he inquired about a blue sedan.

"I don't pay no attention to the cars that go by," the attendant said.

That was to be expected. The bronze man continued onward, the motorcycle not very noisy. He came to a road intersection, the first one of consequence which he had encountered since beginning on the motorcycle. He stopped there, and devoted some time to searching.

It took him half an hour to find a tiny strip of handkerchief with a knot tied near one end.

The bronze man and his assistants had worked together for some time—a very long time, measured by the excitement and danger they had encountered—and they had evolved operating methods to meet most ordinary situations. The inclusion of a code word—always being sure the third word was "today" and the sixth word "feeling" (They varied this code from month to month)—in cablegrams and telegrams was one precaution they had settled upon.

There had been occasions in the past when they had found it necessary to drop bits of cloth as clues. Pieces of cloth lying on the ground are not entirely unusual, and to simplify matters they had agreed to tie a knot near the end of any bits of cloth they dropped which were important. It might be inconvenient to do so, but it avoided confusion.

Doc rode on. Fortunately, there were not many intersecting roads.

It was almost dark when Doc Savage found a knotted cloth fragment which indicated the quarry had turned off the road onto one that was less traveled.

He was near the coast, so close that he could hear the deep-throated bursting of waves against rocky cliffs. He followed the side road. It dipped downward sharply, entering a canyon that was part of an inlet which slashed back from the sea. He crossed a bridge, an old bridge made of logs, with loose plank flooring that rattled.

He could see the tracks of cars now. There were not many. He watched closely.

Where a car had stopped—there were the mark of footprints around it—he stopped the motorcycle and got off to make an examination. He found Long Tom's tracks.

It was no miracle. There was not even anything incredible about being able to identify Long Tom's footprints among many others on the road, because their shoe soles were a composition type with a distinctive marking. That, too, was a convenience which they affected for mutual assistance. They could come upon any jungle or woodland trail and tell at a glance whether one of their companions had gone that way before.

Attention to such small details as this, the acceptance and use of a standardized routine that, while ap-

parently somewhat complicated at first glance, became
a matter of habit, was largely responsible for their having been able to go through such things as they had,
and still remain alive. All of them knew that. Hence
there was no varying from their practice, although
when things were quiet, with no danger threatening, all
those precautions sometimes seemed much on the silly
side.

Long Tom had been conducted along a footpath that
angled up sharply from the right-hand side of the road.

Doc followed the path. Trees crowded closer, shov-
ing out branches so that it was necessary to push
through the foliage. The trail, while distinct, was carpet-
ed with a mat of dead leaves and retained only the
vague outlines of footprints. But here and there bare
ground showed, soft and moist, retaining distinctly the
footprints.

Then Doc found a bit of cloth, a bit of clothing of
the same type which he had been finding from time to
time at intersections as he followed the road.

Suddenly he knew he was falling into a trap.

The cloth wasn't knotted.

The bronze man straightened swiftly. But he had no
chance to act on his discovery.

Jonas, the butler, came out from behind a large
boulder nearby. There was nothing butlerlike about
Jonas now—he wore old khaki pants, flannel shirt and
cap, so that he resembled a native—and there was certainly nothing that left doubts about the rifle he
pointed.

The rifle was an automatic one. It could empty a
clip of several bullets. The caliber was a heavy one
which the maker recommended for any big game in the
world.

"The only reason I don't want to shoot you now is
because the shot might be heard," Jonas said. "That
isn't much of a reason. Hardly anybody lives up here."

His manner was utterly collected and matter-of-fact.

Doc lifted his arms, understanding that he was very
near to death.

Chapter XIV

THE CLIFF

Monk handled the controls of the plane and flew south. They had been north beyond the Canadian border, following the road, and the road had eventually petered out. They had discovered no trace of a blue sedan. Now they were going south again, making another try.

"Look!" Ham exploded.

Monk seized binoculars and stared downward. "Doc's motorcycle!" he said.

He started to dive the plane downward, then quickly changed his mind. He flew on, rather than attract attention to Doc.

Annie Spain asked, "Does he have a portable radio?"

"Yes," Ham said shortly.

Monk explained, "We'll land down the coast somewhere and wait for Doc to call us."

The land offered no opening of sufficient size for them to set the plane down. The ship was big and fast, needed more than an average amount of room.

Monk arched out over the sea and studied that. The waves were small, and there was not much of a swell.

"We'll try the open sea," he said. He waved to the eastward. "Fog rolling in, anyway. It'll hide us."

The fog was thick and close to the sea, like a floating layer of soiled cotton.

They hit, bounced; spray climbed out in sheets. Monk grunted, wrestled the big wheel, batted at the throttles with his palms. The ship straightened out and settled, knocking the tops off a long series of waves before it became stagnant on the surface.

There followed two hours of dreary bouncing around on waves. The motion was nauseating to the extreme. Monk became somewhat green.

There was no radio communication from Doc Savage.

"We better investigate," Monk said biliously.

"Anything so you can get on shore, eh?" Ham quipped. "O.K. But I've been enjoying myself watching you!"

"You would!" Monk snarled. "You better fly this thing."

They took to the air again, climbed in tight circles until they had fifteen thousand feet of altitude. They flew northwest for a while, until the coast appeared in the moonlight.

"There's an inlet close to where we saw Doc's motorcycle," Ham volunteered. "We can land there and make an investigation afoot."

Monk peered downward. His seasickness had subsided. He discerned the inlet, but noted also that it was floored with fog, the cliffs projecting above the layer of vapor and showing the outlines of the cove.

"We'll have to drop down into that fog and land blind," he said. "Suppose we hit a rock."

"There were no rocks," Ham said. "I noticed when we flew past it before."

Annie Spain sat very stiff in the plane during the landing. She knew just enough about flying to be awfully scared. They came down in the fog well out to sea—the motors had been cut at the fifteen-thousand-foot level—and the landing was made dead-stick. Through the fog. Into the mouth of the bay.

The fog rushed past the plane windows, coated the glass until they could see nothing but a gray blur. Monk opened the forward windows, and damp air charged inside. Then they hit the water. It was much calmer here, and the plane eventually slowed until its only motion was that given by the breeze.

"Anchor," Monk said.

"The water is too deep, you ape," Ham objected, then got out the anchor. The water wasn't too deep; only about eight fathoms. The anchor, a small collapsible one designed for gripping properties, took hold and the plane slowly angled its nose into the wind.

Monk put a collapsible boat in the water. It was a little thing, hardly as stable as a canoe. The paddles were of light airplane metal.

"I'll get in first," Annie Spain volunteered, "and hold it for you fellows."

"You aren't going," Ham said.

"You're crazy," Annie Spain snapped.

Ham got a pair of handcuffs out of a compartment. "You're not going anywhere," he said grimly. He walked toward the young woman with the handcuffs.

Monk exploded, "Now wait a minute, Ham! What's the idea of treating this young woman like that?"

"She's been too sassy," Ham said. "And that's only one reason."

"What's another reason?"

"You remember when Long Tom disappeared?" Ham demanded. "Well, this girl locked me in the garage at Sell-'em-short Smith's home about that time, and escaped. She was missing about the time Long Tom vanished. Then she came back."

"She explained her absence," Monk reminded.

"Not to my satisfaction, she didn't. She said she had changed her mind and decided to come back."

"Women change their minds. They're that way."

"Well, I'm not," Ham said. "I'm going to lock her here in the plane while we're gone."

"You idiot!" Monk snapped.

Monk's objections were neither as violent nor as serious as they sounded. He was doing two things—following his usual habit of disapproving of everything

Ham did, and getting in solid with the girl. He noticed she was giving him looks of approval.

"You want to leave her free?" Ham demanded.

"Of course!" Monk said angrily. "She's an honest girl. I believe everything she has told us."

Annie Spain gave Monk a more ravishing smile. Ham saw this, and it scorched him. He suddenly understood why Monk was objecting. So he promptly double-crossed Monk.

"All right," he said. "Here." He handed Monk the handcuffs.

"Huh?" Monk gulped.

"It's up to you," Ham said calmly. "You've outargued me. If she gets handcuffed aboard, you'll have to do it."

Monk knew he had been double-crossed.

"You overdressed shyster!" he gritted.

Monk handcuffed Annie Spain to a cabin brace, where she could sit on the floor in a position that was not uncomfortable.

The young woman parted her lips and let go a round general opinion of them; she did not exactly swear, but her words gave that impression.

"What if this plane sinks, or breaks loose and drifts out to sea?" she demanded.

Monk went to the tool kit, got two small three-cornered files and handed them to her.

"You can file through those handcuff links," the homely chemist said. "I know, because I had to do it once. Take you about three hours if you stay with it. We should be back before then."

They each pocketed one of the small black jars which Doc Savage had instructed them to carry, and discard as soon as they met an enemy.

Then they closed the plane door behind them. The cabin of the plane was practically soundproof, so that the best yelling which Annie Spain would be able to do was not likely to be heard more than a few feet away.

They found Oxalate Smith at the boathouse.

They had been ashore only a few minutes when Oxalate Smith walked out of the darkness, completely astounding them and said, "Oh, gracious, I'm glad to see you!"

The boathouse in itself had been a surprise. There was a long rock running out into the water, and they had climbed onto that without realizing it was a natural wharf which someone had utilized by building a boathouse at the shore end. The boathouse was a very old one, constructed of slabs nailed to the planks, but it was in good repair.

So intense was the darkness that they did not at once recognize Oxalate Smith.

"Oh!" Monk gasped.

He dodged backward so precipitously that he slipped off the rock into the water. Monk was large enough to make quite a splash.

"Sh-h-h!" admonished Oxalate Smith wildly. "They may hear us!"

Ham took a chance and put a flashlight beam on Oxalate Smith. He saw that Oxalate was disheveled, and that he was holding one end of a rope, the other end of which was tied about one of his ankles with a very complicated hard knot.

"Put out the light!" Oxalate Smith exclaimed.

Ham doused the light. "What the devil?" he muttered. "You told us you were an antique dealer and furniture refinisher with a shop in New York."

"Sh-h-h," breathed Oxalate Smith.

There was silence for some moments while they listened, but no sound—no alarming sound, rather, for there was a little noise of night birds—could be detected.

Oxalate Smith whispered, "Remember I told you I frequently made trips into the country to buy antiques at bargain prices?"

"Yes," Ham admitted.

"Well, I was called up here by someone who wanted to sell an original Duncan Phyfe set of furniture. A whole set, mind you! The price named made it a marvelous bargain, if genuine. I rushed right up here. But before that—"

"What happened when you got here?" Ham interrupted.

"Before that, in New York, I was set upon by a footpad," Oxalate Smith went on. "That was right after I left Doc Savage. I do not know what significance that attack had, if any. I was robbed, however. Do you know anything about that attack?"

"Us?" Ham said. "No, we didn't waylay you. And we don't know of anybody who did. You say it was a robber?"

"I didn't catch sight of him. He struck me down in the darkness. Must have sprung upon me and injured me, as well, because my stomach has been bothering me since."

"Your stomach?"

"Yes. It aches slightly. Nothing serious, you understand, but nevertheless uncomfortable."

Monk growled, "Let's skip your bellyache and get down to the present. What happened here?"

"I was made a prisoner."

"When?"

"As soon as I arrived."

"Then what are you doing loose now?"

"I got away. Tonight. I crept down here to this boathouse hoping to find a boat, but there is none. I was wondering how I could escape when I heard you fellows, and realized who you were when one of you spoke."

Monk and Ham digested this amazing story.

"Who seized you?" Monk demanded.

"Why, several men. I had never seen any of them before, with one exception."

"And the exception?"

"Jonas, the butler who was employed by Radiator Smith."

The stillness of the night continued, broken only by the squawking of some predatory sea bird out over the fog-covered water somewhere, and the distant hooting of an owl. Once, far away, a wolf howled, or it might have been a dog, although it sounded like a wolf.

Ham asked, "Have you any idea, Smith, why you were decoyed up here and seized?"

"Well—I have a theory."

"What is it?"

"It was feared that I might identify the master criminal as having been in Radiator Smith's home, and acting strangely."

"Jonas, the butler, you mean?"

"No. He is only a minor crook."

"Who, then?" Ham demanded.

Monk said, "He must mean Annie Spain."

Both Monk and Ham became coldly grim at the thought. They had come to know Annie Spain, and they rather liked her—not entirely, they believed—because she was a remarkably pretty girl. The idea that she was responsible for the deaths horrified them.

"You mean Annie Spain?" Ham asked.

"No," Oxalate Smith said. "I don't mean Annie Spain."

"Who, then?" Ham exploded.

"Radiator Smith himself," said Oxalate Smith.

Monk and Ham digested that; then Monk snorted.

"The idea is ridiculous," Monk said.

"Why? Didn't you know that Maurice Smith wasn't Radiator Smith's true son, but an adopted boy. If Radiator Smith is the criminal, and Maurice found it out, that would give a motive for the murder."

"Um-m-m," Monk said uncertainly.

This possibility had not occurred to either him or Ham earlier.

After a period of silence, Ham changed the subject, asking, "Where were you held a prisoner?"

"In a house on top of the cliff."

"Could we get in it?"

"It might be dangerous," Oxalate Smith said uneasily.

"But we might manage it?"

"Yes."

"Come on," said Monk and Ham together.

Chapter XV

MYSTERY BELOW

It was an ancient house, and big. The first floor was made of native stone, the second was clapboarded, the third shingled. There were gables; against the stars Monk and Ham counted five, and they could see only the side and one end of the structure.

"Sure take a lot of ghosts to haunt that place," Monk offered in a puffing whisper.

The uneasy sobbing of the sea among cliff caves came to them. The house stood not many rods from the lip of the cliff, and the path up which they had climbed had been steep and breath-taking.

There was no light anywhere about the house. No sound. No movement.

"They're still asleep," Oxalate Smith whispered.

"We've got some gas," Ham whispered. "I suggest we use the stuff, then barge in on 'em. Make it simple."

"If there's only six or seven, we can lick 'em bare-handed," said Monk, who liked to fight.

"Don't be a fool," Oxalate Smith whispered.

"He can't help it," Ham said.

The gas—it was an anæsthetic type, producing quick unconsciousness without very harmful aftereffects—was contained in small cylinders equipped with lean spouts through which the stuff could be sprayed, spouts that would penetrate an ordinary keyhole. Monk took the front door, and Ham took the back. They let in plenty of gas.

This gas remained effective for more than thirty

minutes, in which respect it differed from another type of anæsthetic gas which Doc often employed, and which became impotent after it had mingled with the air for less than a minute.

To enter the house, Monk and Ham now employed hoods. These were simply transparent sacks which they pulled over their heads, and which sealed around their necks with an adhesive tape. The sacks were large enough to contain considerable air, but at the best they were only effective for a few minutes. They were, however, the most portable type of mask for emergency use, taking up no more space than a tobacco pouch.

The house was empty.

It took them fifteen minutes of cautious prowling, and three trips inside, before they discovered this.

They rejoined Oxalate Smith outdoors.

"Darn the luck!" Monk muttered. "Where'd they go?"

"Maybe they're out hunting me!" Oxalate Smith gasped. "We had better flee."

"If they're hunting you—right here at the house is the last place they'll look for you," Monk told him. "Let's give the joint the once-over."

As they were starting inside, Oxalate Smith stopped them.

"I have an idea," he said.

"Eh?"

"The men often went into the basement and were gone for long periods," explained Oxalate Smith. "I listened. I think there is some kind of a passage out of the basement. We might find it."

"Now you're talking," Monk said.

As an afterthought purely, Monk extracted his little black jug of a device from his pocket and left it outside, sitting on a window sill where it would be quite noticeable in case Doc Savage reached the house.

There had been a wine vat—or a fish-pickling vat; they never did decide which—in the basement, and this was empty now, and had been for a long time. It was, however, equipped with a bottom which could be dropped in place and sealed, brine or some other liquid afterward being poured into the vat to hide the fact that it was through the bottom that access could be gained to a shaft.

It was not a tunnel. It was a shaft. Sheer, absolutely straight up and down. Round. When they first looked into it, Monk and Ham thought they were peering into the depths of a cistern. But, "Let's look closer!" Oxalate Smith kept urging in a whisper; so they looked, and they found a ladder, a modernistic ladder with iron rungs.

They climbed down for probably fifty feet, Monk first, then Oxalate Smith, then Ham. There was a steady current of air upward, which made Ham feel better.

"If anybody starts down after us," he whispered, "we can just let some gas loose and it will be carried up to them."

"Yeah," Monk said. "But it's what's below that bothers me."

What was below was, first, a large, dark cave of a room. It was natural, they saw; that is, no human agency had excavated it, but rather it was the work of a brook which had, in some prehistoric era, trickled down through the stone and worn channels.

They followed the cave, which became a succession of rooms, each larger than the other and each lower—until finally they came upon the machine.

Monk stared at the machine. "Blazes!" he said.

What he probably meant was that he had never seen such an intricate-looking conglomeration of wheels, coils, tubes, cylinders, belts, cogs, levers—practically everything.

Monk stared at the stuff. Monk was a chemist, an industrial chemist—this was a little different than being a plain chemist, because it necessitated an extra knowledge of modern machinery, mechanical and electrical, and manufacturing processes—but Monk had never seen anything remotely resembling the apparatus below his eyes now. Neither had Ham. But with Ham it was different; he was a lawyer and had dealt more with writs and torts than with transformers and gear ratios.

"What is it?" Ham asked.

"I don't know," Monk said. "It looks like somebody had a dream."

"Well, let's find out."

Monk listened. There seemed to be no one around. He found an electric switch, and turned it, and lights came on. He crouched there, expectant, a super-machine pistol in one hand, a gas grenade in the other, but no one appeared. He looked around.

The simplest part of the contraption stood on the other side of the huge room; moreover, it was the only piece of machinery which seemed to be operating. Monk and Ham moved over to that.

It was like a pistol operating in a cylinder. In this case, the cylinder was a great hole, almost vertical, which water had cut downward through the rock. In the bottom of the hole, the sea churned up and down. There was an opening to the sea down there some-where, funnel-shaped so that each big swell striking the cliff outside drove into the funnel and compressed, so that the water level was raised in the shaft a distance of a score of feet, often more.

The pistol in this unique cylinder was a huge tank of an affair which slid up and down on steel rods, and there was a connecting rod which extended to the machinery on the cave floor.

"A kind of big sea-motor," Ham said.

That explained it as clearly as anything.

Monk stood frowning at the thing, his agile mind trying to calculate roughly how many foot pounds of energy the device was capable of producing. He couldn't tell exactly, of course, but it was plenty. He examined the motor itself. The power was exchanged into electrical energy through the medium of a huge dynamo. From the dynamo, the juice went into—well, Monk wasn't sure what it did go into. The most baffling mess of apparatus he had ever seen, he was certain.

He fooled around the stuff, not touching anything at first, but feeling the urge to do so. It seems to be an in-born trait of the human male that when he sees a complicated machine, he wants to push a button or turn a lever to see what happens. Monk had that impulse. It became overpowering. He started half-reaching for things.

"You better not," Ham said.

"Why not?"

"You remember the lightning that's been striking the Smiths?" Ham asked.

"You think this contraption has got something to do with it?"

"What do *you* think?"

Monk thought it was quite possible, but decided he wouldn't admit it to Ham. He backed away from the electro-mechanical mystery.

"If we had a stick of dynamite," Ham said, "we could fix this golly-wogus, whatever it is."

"I can go back to the plane, get some chemicals and mix us up some nitroglycerin," Monk offered.

It was a good idea, and Ham wondered how he could admit that it was good without going through the disgusting formality of agreeing with Monk.

He was saved the trouble. With no advance warning whatever, men appeared to the side and back of them, men armed with rifles and shotguns. They came out quickly, in a way that showed that they had been there the whole time, and had only been waiting to make sure no one else accompanied Monk, Ham and Oxalate Smith.

Monk and Ham promptly whipped out their super-machine pistols. They got them pointed. But they didn't fire. It was perfectly obvious that they would get a few shots out of the weapons, but would certainly be shot down themselves. And there was a difference be-

tween their ammunition and that of their enemies—
they were shooting the unconsciousness-producing type
of slug commonly called a "mercy" bullet.

"Think it over, you guys," Monk warned grimly.
"These guns put out a lot of lead in a little time."

There was silence, except for the churning of the big
sea-power engine behind them.

"I am going to move," one of the men said. "I am
going to show you something."

The man moved away, and came back carrying a
device contained in a greenish metal box about the size
of a common suitcase. It was so heavy that he had a
little trouble carrying it.

He placed the box on the floor, turned a lever and
one end dropped open, disclosing a black panel on
which there was a round brassy-looking disk. There
was a switch on top of the box. The man threw that.

He stepped back.

"Something is going to happen," he said. "Be careful
your guns don't go off by accident."

Monk opened his mouth, shut it, asked, "I don't
get—"

Cr-r-r-a-a-c-k! It was terrific. And blinding. For a
lightning bolt—unmistakably that was what it was—
came out of the box and jumped toward them. Monk
thought at first he had been struck. But no! He whirled
to Ham. Ham was all right.

But Oxalate Smith wasn't. He folded down on the
floor, making no sound, and lay there.

"You killed him!" Monk squalled.

"Yes," the man said calmly, "we killed him. He was
useless to us. But you aren't."

Monk tightened his muscles, swung his super-
machine pistol toward the speaker.

"Wait!" the man rapped. "You've got a chance of
staying alive!"

"Yeah," Monk said coldly. "I bet it's a fat chance."
The homely chemist was going to start fighting. Ham
realized it, and understood that they had no chance
whatever. "Wait!" Ham gasped. He seized Monk's

arm. Monk snarled, struck at him. But Ham forced Monk's arm up, and when the pistol blared out deafeningly, the bullets did nothing but splatter their chemical contents against the ceiling.

The men with the guns rushed them, bore them down under a wave of fists and clubbing gunstocks.

Chapter XVI

GIRL TREACHEROUS

Annie Spain would not want to see another file during the rest of her life. The sound of it, as she rasped it back and forth over her handcuff links, had long since ceased merely to set her teeth on edge. The sound was stabbing at her brain now, maddening her. But she was almost through the links.

When she did get the link separated, she wrenched herself free of the brace in the plane cabin and lurched to her feet. She fell immediately. In the concentrated effort of using the file, she had forgotten to move about, so that she was stiff. She clamped her teeth together, got up again, and weaved to the plane door.

There was no boat. No way of getting ashore except swimming. She clambered down on the float and put one of her feet in the water.

"Brr!" she said, and shivered.

She debated pulling up the anchor and letting the plane drift ashore, but dismissed that idea. The plane would be wrecked on the rocks, probably. She didn't want that.

Searching the plane cabin, she found a gun—it was a common automatic pistol, the operation of which she understood, and not one of the intricate supermachine pistols—and ran a cord through the trigger guard of the weapon and tied it, as best she could, on top of her head. She tried to tie a box of cartridges there, but it would not stay; she compromised by greasing the cartridges thoroughly with a can of grease which she found in the tool locker, and stowing them inside the front of her blouse. She put a small flashlight there, also, after noting that it appeared to be waterproof.

She got her bearings by the wind, and slid into the water. It was cold enough to stab her all over like needles. She struck out, glad that she was a good swimmer, and for the first few minutes she was plagued by a horrible fear she would not make it, but as her muscles generated heat from the exercise, she was more confident.

When she reached shore, she took off her wet things and wrung them out as best she could. The automatic had not gotten very wet; she took out the clip and blew into the mechanism and into the barrel to get most of the water out. She had heard that it did not hurt modern cartridges to get them wet, but she was not too sure.

She had studied the lay of the ground from the plane before dark; she knew there was a big house on a hill, but it was some distance, three quarters of a mile or so from the spot where they had seen Doc Savage's motorcycle.

Her first move, she decided, would be to see whether the bronze man's motorcycle was still there.

It was a long trip, a rough one. Being a woman, Annie hated it thoroughly, because it hopelessly ruined her suit, which she had bought from one of New York's swankiest woman's shops, paying plenty. She did not use her flashlight.

Doc Savage and Jonas were at the motorcycle. She heard their voices—Jonas demanding to know the whereabouts of the rest of his men, and the bronze man either ignoring the inquiries, or refusing to answer.

Annie Spain took a chance; she thumbed on her flashlight.

"Grab high!" she said sharply.

Jonas was standing. He held an automatic rifle, but he let it fall instantly.

Doc Savage half lay, half sat on the ground, with ropes around his ankles and wrists. He was tied very securely, Annie Spain saw.

"Stand still!" she warned.

She went over and got the automatic rifle which Jonas had dropped, pulled back the slide to make sure there was a cartridge in the chamber, then exchanged that weapon for her automatic, fearing the cartridges in the automatic might be wet and useless.

"Don't think I won't shoot you," she advised Jonas coolly.

She was busy a moment with her thoughts. There was a length of rope lying beside the motorcycle, some that had been left over when Jonas tied the bronze man.

Annie Spain picked up the rope.

"I better separate you two," she said. To Jonas, she commanded, "Get moving. Walk up the path. And one wrong jump out of you will be your last."

She sounded coldly earnest.

Jonas swallowed. "I . . . I—"

"Get going!" said the girl.

Jonas shuffled away. She followed him. She said, "I ought to shoot you down!" in a rather loud and determined voice.

They moved along the path perhaps a hundred yards.

The girl spoke in a much different voice.

"How are things going?" she asked.

Jonas stopped. In a friendly tone, he said, "Well, I was waiting there, hoping you would turn up. I been hoping to see you for hours, knowing you were with Savage."

"Does Savage suspect me?"

"A little."

"Does he suspect we're in cahoots?"

"Oh, no."

"That's nice," said Annie Spain. "That's swell. And you've been doing nice work, Jonas."

"Thank you, miss."

"You don't need to act like a servant. We are partners in this. You'll be a millionaire."

"I hope so, miss. Thank you."

"When I found out you were one of the gang, I had a talk with you and you decided to work for me. That makes us partners."

"Yes, miss."

"And it'll also make you a dead man if those others find out about it before we're ready."

"I know."

"Is this their—ah, factory, you might call it?" Annie Spain asked.

"Yes, miss. There is a big house on the hill, and caves in the cliff below that. The ... er ... 'factory' is a good word for it—is there."

"Can we raid the place?"

"We can try, miss. I hid a machine gun under the porch. We can get that."

"Are you game to try it?"

"Yes, miss. The thought of making a million dollars makes me very game indeed, if you'll pardon my saying so."

"It will be more than a million, Jonas. You go up to the house. I'll meet you there later. Meantime, I will get rid of Doc Savage."

"Begging your pardon miss, but are you going to kill him?"

"No, Jonas. If we fail in our raid on the ... er ... factory, we may need help. Doc Savage is the very best kind of help."

"Yes, miss. I agree with you. There is a mine tunnel with a very strong door along the cove shore. You cannot miss it."

"Mine tunnel?"

"Yes. To imprison Savage, miss."

They separated, Jonas moving off up the hill, Annie Spain returning to Doc Savage.

The bronze man had been working at his ropes, and he had nearly succeeded in liberating himself. Annie

Spain hastily dropped beside the bronze man, seized the knots and untied them, liberating Doc.

"I let Jonas get away," she said. "Deliberately."

"Why?" Doc asked.

"I scared him."

"You—"

"So bad that he told me the truth, as much of it as he knew. He told me where the gang has their hideout. And he told me nobody is there, and we can walk right in and take over their infernal machine."

Doc inquired, "Did he tell you who is the brains behind this?"

"He didn't know. None of them know. It's a mystery."

"But he told you what their—infernal machine, you called it—is like?"

"Yes. He said it was a marvelous invention for committing murder. It is electrical in nature. I'm not technical enough to understand it. Jonas didn't understand it either, for that matter."

"I see," Doc said. "And you say we can seize this machine?"

"Yes."

"Where?"

"I'll show you," Annie Spain said. "It's right along the shore of the cove. It's a kind of a tunnel—an old abandoned mine tunnel."

"All right, show me," Doc said.

They moved through the darkness, Annie Spain leading the way down to the cove edge and along the shore, wondering if she would be able to find the mine tunnel. Jonas had said she couldn't miss it, but she was worried.

The cove had no beach worthy of the name—the patches of sand here and there among the rocks could hardly qualify as beach—and the going was very difficult. Also it was slow, because they had to travel without making too much noise. The fog swirled around them like streamers of gray cheesecloth.

The tunnel was perhaps fifty feet up the face of the

sloping cove bank from the water, and loose débris taken from the tunnel when it was dug had been dumped outside, making a long slide down to the shore.

The tunnel mouth was blackly forbidding.

"They may be in there—Jonas could have been mistaken," the girl said.

"Or maybe Jonas came back and warned them."

"I don't think he did."

Doc Savage said, "We had better be careful. I'll tell you what—you go back fifty feet or so and conceal yourself while I investigate."

"All right," Annie Spain said. "I will whistle like this"—she whistled once softly, an excellent likeness of a whippoorwill call—"to warn you if anybody comes."

"Right."

Doc Savage located the young woman some distance away from the tunnel mouth, left her there, and moved back toward the dark opening in the earth.

Annie Spain did not remain where she had been left any longer than it required the bronze man to reach the tunnel. Then she crept forward, reached the tunnel mouth, and explored cautiously with her hands.

Jonas had said there would be a door. There was. It was made of wood, steel-plated, and even stronger than she had hoped.

"Doc Savage!" the young woman called softly.

Doc's voice came to her so faintly and hollowly that she knew he was far back in the mine tunnel.

"What is it?" the bronze man asked.

Annie Spain laughed. She slammed the heavy door, closing the bronze man inside the tunnel, and locked it with the heavy padlock she had found hooked in the hasp.

Chapter XVII

THE CHANGE OF MIND

Annie Spain reached the top of the hill and found the big old house with the many gables. After she had searched cautiously for a time, she located the erstwhile butler, Jonas.

"Over here, miss," Jonas hissed, so she could find them.

"I took care of Doc Savage," Annie Spain whispered.

"What did you do with him?"

"In the mine tunnel, like you said."

"Are you sure he is in there?"

"Oh, yes indeed. He called to me from far back in the tunnel just before I slammed and locked the door."

"Good."

"It'll be good if there's no other exit from that mine tunnel. You are sure of that?"

"Oh, yes, miss. Positive," said Jonas.

They moved close to the house, so that its bulk shoved up above them, a rather shapeless thing against the stars, but a thing of formidable magnitude. The sound of the sea came to them, sighings and coughings of the waves flinging against the cliff. Closer at hand, the wind stirred leaves and occasionally whimpered among the many gables of the big house.

"Where is everybody?" Annie Spain demanded.

"Down below. In the cliff cavern I was telling you about."

"Where is the machine gun?"

"Over there, miss." Jonas conducted her to the porch and got down on all fours and disappeared under the flooring, to come out a moment later with a bulky object wrapped in a cloth, an article which proved to be a hand machine gun when he uncovered it. There were extra drums of ammunition.

"All right," the girl said. "Let's start our rat-hunt."

Jonas conducted her inside. He volunteered some information in a whisper.

"He has always owned this house," he said, "and his father and grandfather before him. It is a very old house."

Annie Spain asked, "How did he come to invent the contraption?"

"He is a very brilliant man, you know. He was educated in the finest universities here and abroad. I think that may be one of his troubles—too much education. Something is wrong with him. He has no human qualities whatever, once you know him well."

"Did he invent the gadget here?"

"Yes, miss, I think so. It took years, I understand. I think he started the work in Europe, then came back to this country when all that trouble started over there. Perhaps they ran him out of Europe. I don't know."

"Why work in a cave?" Annie Spain asked.

"You don't understand, miss. A great deal of power is necessary. The equivalent of thousands and thousands of horsepower. He rigged a kind of sea-power motor in the cliff, and got the power that way. He is a genius, miss, but not normal in mind."

"I know," Annie Spain said. "He's crazy for power."

"Yes, indeed."

They reached the basement shaft that extended down from the bottom of the vat, and stood there peering into the depths uneasily, listening to make sure no one was immediately below to hear them once they started down.

"Crazy for power," Annie Spain repeated. "Yes, that describes him. You know, Jonas, that he came to me when he was assembling his gang and wanted to hire me as one of them."

"Yes, I know."

"I guess my reputation as an adventuress fooled him into thinking I would work for anybody. I had just gotten out of that spy mess in Austria, and there was lots of publicity. I was painted as a Mata Hari and Dracula combination, sort of."

Jonas said, "I don't hear anyone down below, miss."

"I pumped him when he tried to hire me," Annie Spain said grimly, "and found out what a wonderful invention he had developed. He wanted to use it to terrify people, to rule a lot of big business enterprises, and finally—the United States."

"Yes, miss. He's power-crazy."

"I think I was justified in turning on him and trying to take his infernal machine away from him, because he was going to kill people." The young woman smiled slightly. "Of course, I wasn't doing it as a good deed, entirely. I know that machine itself is worth millions if I can get it."

Jonas, the butler, moved his shoulders uneasily. He felt, when he was in the presence of Annie Spain, rather as if he was associating with a man-eating tigress. The young woman was so competent, so unafraid, that she scared him.

They began, with infinite care, to climb down the shaft, Jonas going first on the ladder, the girl coming close above him and keeping the machine gun balanced on his shoulder, both of them going very slowly because they felt heavy and awkward with the ammunition drums stowed in their clothing. The drums were heavy.

Jonas reached the bottom first. There was a little light, enough to show the tight ring of figures that surrounded the foot of the shaft.

Jonas made a slight gesture at the men, then tossed one of them the machine gun.

"It's all right," he told the girl, who was still out of sight in the shaft.

But just to make sure there was no slip in capturing her, he seized one of her ankles and jerked. Annie Spain fell down the last steps of the shaft to the cave floor.

Men sprang upon her and gripped her arms. She tried to fight them, but did not have much success.

"So you sold out on me!" she told Jonas grimly.

"Not exactly, miss," Jonas said. "You never hired me in the first place, although you didn't know that. We simply thought it advisable for me to pretend to work with you. It made everything much safer for us, you see."

A man said, "Where is Doc Savage?"

Jonas turned. "Locked in the old mine tunnel. Miss Spain locked him there."

Annie Spain let them tie her wrists and ankles—there was hardly anything else she could have done—and remained where they dropped her at one side of the chamber. She watched them prepare a party to go after Doc Savage. Her mouth was tight, and her body felt colder than the stone against which she crouched. They would not hesitate to kill a woman; there was no doubt whatever in her mind about that. It was not the first time that death had seemed in prospect, but it seemed more certain now than at any time in the past. Certain. She saw no way of avoiding it.

Jonas, even in his present triumph, was still the perfect butler—smug, polite, using a modulated voice in which there was just a trace of pride.

He led the men up the shaft, out of the house and down the steep slope toward the cove shore and the old tunnel. They went boldly, lighting their way with flashlights. There was nothing to be afraid of. Doc Savage, his three men, Annie Spain, all had been captured.

Jonas unlocked the heavy iron door of the mine tunnel. It was intact, he saw.

"Come out!" he warned.

After about five minutes of trying to get someone to

come out of the tunnel, they ventured inside. The place was empty.

Moreover, the floor inside the door was muddy, and they could see that there were no tracks in the mud, a good indication that Doc Savage had never even entered the tunnel.

Chapter XVIII

THE BAD BREAK

The ventriloquist known as the Great Lander had taught the bronze man more than the art of "throwing" the voice, which was nothing more than speaking so that the voice did not sound as if it came from the speaker; he had taught Doc to imitate other voices, and make them seem to come from very far away.

So now Doc stood in the darkness near the tunnel mouth.

"Monk!" he called. "Monk! Ham! Are you there?"

It sounded as if he were more than a quarter of a mile away.

He changed to Monk's voice, said, "Over here, Doc. We been looking for you! Over here by the end of the cove."

Jonas heard the voices, and he was taken in. He swore in a harsh tone full of horror.

"Damn!" he gasped. "That Monk and Ham got away! And Savage is loose!"

"They're back toward the end of the cove," a man growled.

"Come on!" Jonas snapped.

The men moved away, bunched tightly, guns ready, and not showing their flashlights.

Doc let them go. He had not entered the old mine tunnel at any time. When Annie Spain had thought she heard him call to her from far back in the tunnel, the bronze man had actually been outside, only a few feet from the girl.

The fact that Annie Spain had expected the bronze man to be in the tunnel had made the deception easy. In ventriloquism, having the audience expect the voice to come from another source was half the battle. Otherwise ventriloquists would not have a dummy to sit on their knee.

Having sidetracked a part of the enemy temporarily, Doc climbed up the cliff to the house.

Like Monk and Ham when they had first come there, he had no idea of the layout of the place. He spent some time cautiously prowling the outside, listening at the windows. The moonlight was brighter, so that he had to keep low in the weeds that surrounded the place to remain inconspicuous.

He saw the small black jug which Monk had placed on the window sill. He got it, opened it.

The contrivance was a tiny recording electroscope —a device that registered the presence in its neighborhood of radioactive substances.

Doc had designed several of them as protective apparatus for hospitals in which a store of infinitely valuable radium was kept; the jugs, when planted in the doorways of the hospitals, and hooked to an electrical relay and bell, would raise an alarm the moment anyone attempted to pass through the door with any of the hospital's radium.

They were sensitive enough, these electroscopes, to register the passing of anyone who had merely been treated with radium emanation. There was an adjustment which could be screwed down to prevent this. In the present case the adjustment was not screwed down, however.

Doc examined the electroscope. It showed that it had been close to a slightly radioactive substance.

Doc reached the vat in the basement. Doc stared down the shaft. Far below, he could see light, and occasionally there were small sounds of men moving about. He saw a man shove his head into the shaft and jerk back quickly so as not to be seen. They were watching the thing.

Doc retreated. He left the basement—the basement was no place to spend much time, for he could be trapped there—and got out of the house.

The yard had a crop of weeds that looked like monkey fur, and there were clumps of scrawny shrubbery which had been planted there but never trimmed. The bronze man took shelter in that maze.

He had not been there long when there was the pounding noise of frantic feet and the whipping of branches flung aside. Two men. They were in a great hurry.

Jonas and one other, it proved to be. They reached the house, panting.

"I'll go down and get help," Jonas puffed. "Harry, you stay here and watch—if you're not afraid to. If you're not afraid, understand?"

"Afraid!" the other man said rather angrily. "What do you mean?"

"No offense, Harry," Jonas said. "I'm not telling you to stay here on guard—it's dangerous, because Doc Savage and his two men are around somewhere."

The other man hesitated. He did not like the idea of remaining up here alone, but the question of whether he had the courage was at stake, so that he did not have much choice.

"I'll stay," he growled.

Jonas disappeared into the house. The guard Harry leaned against a porch post, rifle tucked under his arm.

Doc Savage moved cautiously, taking advantage of such sounds as the wind made stirring the weeds and bushes. Whenever his fingers found rocks, he picked them up, until he had three small pebbles and a larger rock, a stone about the size of half a brickbat, in his hands.

He flicked two pebbles to the left of the guard. Harry whirled toward the sound.

Doc lifted and let fly the larger rock, throwing with great care. He made a hit; the man's head was not a difficult target. Harry dropped. The rock bounded around on the porch, making some noise.

Doc Savage raced forward, leaned over and clipped the man with his fist to lengthen the period of unconsciousness. He searched Harry, found some coins, a short pencil, a few letters in envelopes, a pocket knife and a flashlight. Doc took those. He dragged Harry into the brush and boldly began descending the shaft.

Jonas was only a short distance below.

"What's wrong, Harry?" he growled.

Doc imitated fairly well the voice of the guard he had just knocked senseless.

"I got scared," he said gruffly. "I'm going down with you."

The hollow acoustics of the shaft further distorted the voice so that the deceit worked. Jonas climbed on down. Doc descended directly behind him.

The critical moment came when Jonas reached the bottom and stepped clear.

Without following him out, Doc said, in the guard's voice, "I'm gonna wait here in the shaft and keep a watch."

Jonas growled something unflattering about men with no nerve, but he was too concerned with his own troubles for suspicion to occur to him. He galloped away.

Doc dug out the pencil he had found on Harry, and one of the envelopes, on which he printed:

Jonas:
I changed my mind and climbed back to watch from the house.

Harry

He folded the envelope and hooked it over one of the metal ladder rungs so that it could hardly remain undiscovered.

The bronze man trailed Jonas cautiously.

He did not continue following Jonas, however. Jonas swung right, into a room where a number of men waited. Doc took a left turn, because he had seen the chamber which Monk and Ham had earlier discovered, the room filled with fantastic machinery.

The machinery was running now. There was a shaded electric bulb over a large instrument panel, and this gave some vague light.

Doc began with the source of power that utilized the surge of waves in the pit, and moved his attention quickly to the more intricate array of mechanism.

He was careful not to venture too close to the conglomeration of apparatus. There was a yellow circle painted on the floor around the machinery, he noted, and he was careful not to venture inside that. He stared with interest at various devices, endeavored to follow circuits with his eyes, and identify the apparatus into which they entered. Many of the electrodes and conductors were surrounded with a visible corona, due to the enormous frequency of the current which they carried.

Abruptly the bronze man showed a new interest.

Outside, he heard a bustle of movement. Going to the aperture between the two caves—the chambers were actually not rooms, but rather different arms of the underground labyrinth—and watching around the sharp angle, he saw that Jonas had assembled another group of men and they were preparing to leave.

"You're sure Monk and Ham haven't escaped?" Jonas demanded angrily.

"You can see for yourself," a man said.

"I'll do that."

Jonas strode down a narrow passage, dropped a board that spanned a deep pit with water at the bottom, gingerly crossed over and scowled at a guard who stood there.

"Let me see the prisoners," he growled.

"Sure." The cell guard turned, thumbed on the beam of a flashlight.

Monk, Ham, Long Tom and Annie Spain were

staked out. The floor of the cave at that point was gray clay that had washed in through the ages, and long iron pipes had been driven into this, forming anchorages to which the prisoners were spread-eagled.

Jonas stared at them.

"But I heard their voices outside," he growled. "Heard Savage, too."

He rubbed his jaw, scraped fingers through his hair, and his mouth made thinking shapes. Suddenly his face blanched. Scared wordless, he dashed back to the shaft which led up to the house on the cliff rim.

Jonas saw the note. He read it. Then he demonstrated that his intelligence was past the ordinary.

"Savage is in here!" he roared. "Get your guns! Get all the lights on!"

Chapter XIX

THE STOMACH TROUBLE

Doc was moving fast by then. The guard had rushed away from the prisoners to see what the excitement was about. Doc reached the board over the pit. The board was an ingenius but simple door for a prison; once it was hauled back, it made the place a perfect jail, since the coming-out end was much higher than the other, high enough that no man was likely to leap that gap and at the same time mount the distance. The height alone was a good high jump.

It took all of Doc's great strength to get the board down without attracting attention. He whipped across silently. He brought out the pocketknife he had taken from Harry as he crossed, made one big circular slash and got Monk free.

"Loosen the others," the bronze man said swiftly.

He spun, went back the way he had come. His leaps were long with haste. He crossed the plank, veered right, took to shadows. Farther up the cavern, lights were coming on, their luminance leaping through the passages like bright monsters. But here there were shadows that could conceal him.

He reached the great room where the machinery grumbled and whined. Earlier inspection had shown him how the sea-power motor could be stopped—there was a big lever that actuated a clutch. He threw that. The big device went silent; gears stopped grinding, generators ceased to whine, and the spark-blue corona disappeared from around the myriad of conductors. Then there was a report, sharp and terrific, like a bolt of lightning, and a jagged rope of flame climbed briefly through the apparatus.

Evidently that was the wrong way to shut it off. Some smoke and odor of burned insulation oozed into the room.

Doc did not wait. He pitched for a darkened niche, a place closed by an iron-barred grille. The grille was not locked; he jerked it open—there was a squawk of rusty hinges as he did so—and dashed his flashlight beam over the contents.

They were metal cases that might have been suitcases, for they were equipped with carrying handles. But they were not suitcases, the bronze man knew.

He clamped his lips, advanced on the cases. He was scared. He knew that he was closer to death now than possibly at any time in his rather hair-raising career. There was death in each one of those boxes; it was disaster of a concentrated kind that could kill scores at once, unless he was mistaken. And a single false move on his part would release it.

He began working on one of the cases. There was a switch on each of them; he was careful not to close it. Instead, he worked on the contacts, was soon elated to discover what he had feared would be a tedious job could be made a quick one. The wire from one contact came away from the contact—it was soldered to the jaws of the switch—and entered the box through a small hole, bushed with an insulating compound, perhaps half an inch away.

He could thrust his belt buckle under the wire, tear it loose, then grip the wire with his fingers and pull it until it broke, thus making a quick repair out of the question.

He went over six of the boxes in this fashion. There were seven of them. Doc picked up the seventh box, backed out of the recess, and a man shot at him.

It was too dark for the fellow who fired the shot to take a decent aim, and the bullet missed. But the man yelled an alarm.

"Get the lights on in the power room!" Jonas squalled.

"I can't!" the man howled back. "All the lights came off the switchboard. He could shoot me before I got there!"

That gave Doc Savage an idea. He ducked back into the barred recess. There was an electric bulb hanging from a dropcord and he seized it, put his flashlight on the bulb and examined it.

Thirty-two volts. It was a thirty-two volt bulb, not a one-hundred-ten-volt one. This meant that power for the lights came from a battery supply.

He picked up rocks—there were plenty lying about—and went back to a spot where he could see the switchboard without getting in range of the guns. He threw his rocks. Two of them missed, but the third, thrown very hard, smashed a master fuse out of its mounting and there was sudden darkness all through the cavern.

Doc moved fast then. He figured he might stand a chance of reaching his associates; if he could ever stand a chance, now was the time.

But a voice halted him.

It was an urgent, squeaking voice.

"Mr. Savage," it said. "Help me!"

It came from the right. Doc went over.

"Mr. Savage," the voice said, almost sobbing.

Doc thumbed on the flashlight quickly.

Oxalate Smith lay on the floor. Apparently he had been concealed in a dark corner, and at the outbreak of the excitement had crawled out into the open.

"Put out the light!" he gasped.

"They can't see us here," Doc said. "What are you doing here?"

"They decoyed me up here from New York," Oxalate Smith said rapidly. "Then they captured me, and tried to kill me with their infernal machine. They hit me with a bolt of lightning. They thought I was dead. Your men think I am dead. But I'm not."

It was obvious he was far from dead.

"Can you walk?" Doc demanded.

"Maybe I can. I was afraid I couldn't. That is why I called you." Oxalate Smith sounded frantic. "Take me with you."

"Take you with us where?"

"When you escape."

Doc said, "Come on."

The bronze man leaned over then, lifted Oxalate Smith to his feet. Then he clamped his left arm around Oxalate Smith's neck, jamming the man to his chest helplessly.

Doc picked up the metal case with the other hand.

He walked toward the open part of the cave.

"Watch out," Doc yelled. "I'm holding Oxalate Smith in front of me."

Oxalate Smith went through several convulsions, then began to kick frantically at Doc's legs, causing the bronze man agony.

Doc loosened Oxalate's throat, held him by an arm about the chest, an arm that confined the fellow's arms like a steel band. Oxalate could yell now.

"Don't shoot!" Oxalate squalled. "Rush the damned fool! But don't shoot! He's got me!"

Doc obligingly turned a flashlight beam on Oxalate Smith's face so that the men could see that Oxalate was really a prisoner. Then he ran toward Monk and the others.

"Monk!" he called.

"Over here!" Monk barked.

Behind Doc, there was shouting—yells intended to bring all the members of the gang from the various parts of the cliff cave.

Monk galloped up, trailed closely by Ham, Long Tom and Annie Spain.

"Who's this?" Monk gasped, pointing at Doc's prisoner.

"Oxalate Smith."

"Oxalate—but he's dead! We saw them strike him with lightning."

Doc said, "You saw them make a pretense of that. Probably the charge jumped to a nearby electrode instead of Oxalate's body, and he just fell over and played dead."

"Then he's one of them?"

"He's more than that," Doc said.

The bronze man was moving while he spoke. He headed toward the higher portions of the cavern, the spot where the shaft led upward to the house.

But flight was cut off. Someone fired at them—four rapid shots from an automatic—and Ham made a snarling sound and fell down, but jumped up immediately. He clamped a hand to the calf of his leg. Crimson leaked through his fingers.

"Back," Doc said. "Even if we did get to that shaft, they would kill us while we were climbing it."

They retreated. They had no arms, except what rocks they had picked up. In the darkness these were not entirely useless. But suddenly the lights came on. They had found the switchboard in the power room.

"Run!" Doc rapped. "Back to the prison!"

"But—"

"It's the safest place," Doc rapped. "We can pull in the board and keep them from reaching us temporarily."

Ham was running—he was ignoring his wound—well ahead of the others. He rounded a corner, almost ran into the muzzle of a rifle. He twisted so that, although the gun exploded, the bullet missed him. He fell upon the rifle, twisting furiously, going over and over with his foe, concentrating on getting the weapon.

Monk rushed in, leaned down with a fist. The foe made a single barking sound and stretched out motionless.

"You better take it easy, with that hole in your leg," Monk warned.

"Shut up and see if he's got any cartridges," Ham ordered.

Then suddenly an avalanche of figures were upon them. Seven or eight men, desperately intent.

"Don't use your guns!" Oxalate Smith screamed.

Doc Savage jammed the metal case into Ham's hands, said, "Get it across the board into the place where you were held prisoner."

Ham nodded, fled with the box.

The fight lasted a minute or two, and during the interval no one probably had a coherent thought. Everything was by instinct. Strike, clutch, kick—anything to get a foe down.

Oxalate Smith got up and ran. Doc could not hold him and fight at the same time. The bronze man slugged Oxalate once, and the man dropped, feigning unconsciousness—Doc suspected he had not hit the man hard enough, but had no time to remedy it—then Oxalate crawled away, got up and ran.

Suddenly there was quiet. Not silence—just no more action for the moment. Of the men on the floor, three were moaning and one kept screaming over and over with the agony of a broken arm.

"The prison niche," Doc rapped.

They ran, feeling better now, for they had rifles and some ammunition.

"Look," Monk barked, stopping. "Here's Ham!"

Ham was not out. He had been clubbed over the head.

"Some guy grabbed the box from me," he said. "But he didn't get away with it—I managed to kick it into the pit. It fell in the water down there somewhere."

"Come on," Doc said.

They crossed the board. They hauled the plank back, giving them at least temporary sanctuary.

The bronze man searched quickly. He had noticed that this arm of the cave turned sharply, and went back some distance—far enough to offer them protection from both bullets and hand grenades.

Ham sank down on the floor. He was weak from his wound.

"At any rate," he said grimly, "I kicked that box into the pit. They won't get it."

Doc said, "I hope you knew what you were kicking around."

"You sound as if I had kicked a case of nitroglycerin," Ham said.

"Worse."

"Eh?"

"That case," Doc said, "probably contained more electricity than has ever been condensed in one container before." The bronze man turned to Annie Spain. "That is right, isn't it?"

"That," said Annie Spain, "is about it. It works like a storage battery and a Leyden jar, only different, and more so. Instead of storing eighty or a hundred ampere hours of current, as in an automobile storage battery, for instance, this thing will store hundreds of millions."

The young woman stared at them, waiting for them to understand just how important this was.

"You realize what a tremendous thing this is, don't you?" she demanded. "A steamship—the *Queen Mary*, for instance—will merely put one of those storage cases full of electricity aboard, and cross and recross the Atlantic. Planes can fly around the world non-stop with electric motors, probably."

Monk said. "So that's why you tried to steal it?"

"Yes," Annie Spain said. "Maybe I was a crook. But at least I was trying to steal the secret from a man who was going to use it to murder people. I wasn't intending to murder anyone. I was going to sell it to industry."

Doc asked quietly, "When you were conferring with Oxalate Smith, when he first tried to enlist you in his gang, did he explain why he had decided to commit murder with his discovery, instead of selling it to science?"

"He's crazy for power. That's why."

"But he didn't explain?"

"No."

Monk said, "Wait a minute! Oxalate Smith! Was he the master mind?"

"Yes—Oxalate Smith," Doc Savage said.

"But how did you know?"

Doc said, "The first time we captured Oxalate Smith, I let him go, then set upon him in a darkened alley so he would not recognize me. I overpowered him, knocked him out, and while he was unconscious, forced a mildly radioactive compound into his stomach. It was a harmless compound which would not digest, which would form a lump too large to pass from the stomach, and therefore would remain there."

"He's been complaining of a bellyache," Monk said. "I guess your radioactive stuff gave it to him. But what was the idea?"

"To plant electroscopes which would register the presence of the radioactive material."

"You mean—"

"Yes, once in the building on Broadway in New York City, where Long Tom left his electroscope. It told me Oxalate Smith was there in the room. Hence he was the leader, because the leader spoke from the room."

"But during the fight after they found Long Tom, others came in—"

"That fight was near the door," Doc said, "far enough away not to affect the electroscope. Later, at the house on this cliff, Monk's electroscope told me Oxalate Smith was not only here, but had gone in and out of the house a number of times recently. Therefore, when he told me he had been lying dazed in the cave, I knew it was not the truth."

"So Oxalate Smith is the main cheese," Long Tom muttered.

"Speaking of the devil," Monk called, "here he is."

Monk was watching the entrance.

Oxalate Smith did not show himself. Monk was nursing the stock of his rifle against his cheek, hoping the man would be that much of a fool. Monk did not share Doc's scruples against injuring anyone, even an enemy, if it could be helped.

Oxalate Smith yelled at them.

"Come out of there, one at a time," he shouted, "and you will be safe. Send Long Tom Roberts out first."

Long Tom snorted.

"You gotta give him credit for persistence," he muttered. "He thinks I'm rich. So he's still trying to get me."

Doc called, "None of us are coming out."

Long Tom had an inspiration.

"Furthermore," Long Tom bellowed, "Doc brought down a portable radio transmitter and we're going to use that to summon help. You haven't got a chance, and you know it."

Oxalate Smith swore, shook his fist at them. The instant the fist appeared, Monk fired at it. It was impossible to tell whether he hit it, because Oxalate Smith's cursing could not have become louder.

"I'm not sure that was wise," Doc said.

"If I could've shot him between the eyes, it would have been wiser," Monk said.

"I did not mean that. I meant Long Tom's fib that we have a radio."

"Eh?"

"It will make them desperate. They will not give us time that they might otherwise have given us."

Long Tom growled sheepishly, "I never thought of that."

They realized suddenly that Oxalate Smith was retreating. They could hear his voice, ordering his men into spots where they could prevent the prisoners escaping.

Doc was abruptly concerned.

"Smith!" he called loudly. "Oxalate Smith!"

"Yes."

"Do not try to use one of those electrical containers on us."

Oxalate Smith laughed, a mirthless sound that was completely ugly and determined.

"You guessed it," he said.

The explosion—it was quite deafening—came possibly five minutes later. It was not exactly an explosion, but rather a concussion caused by air rushing into a vacuum created by a fabulous electrical discharge—at least, this was Long Tom's opinion.

There were lights as well. Not ordinary lights, but the unearthly, unpredictable display of coldly fantastic blues and slashing yellows that characterize high-frequency electrical phenomena.

The blast must have been all the suitcase-shaped containers discharging at once. One of them had probably been switched on, and failing to work, someone had tried to investigate, with the result that the charge had been released, setting off all the others.

The released electricity, millions and millions of volts at high amperage, behaved weirdly. It balled up in great tub-sized sizzling monsters of green flame and leaped around on the floor. It became long greenish snakes that made whizzing noises and bounced around on the ceiling or crawled along the walls.

A quick change took place in the air. There was suddenly odor, the smell of ozone, and of things burned. The walls became charged, and suddenly two charges got together with a deafening crash, spanning a gap between two stone walls.

Ordinarily, an electric discharge is over in a moment. But this one persisted for—it seemed like minutes—several seconds.

After it was over, the guards, all but two who had been shocked into insensibility by the discharge, got up and ran away.

That cleaned it up. Except for a development that made Annie Spain feel rather foolish.

"One of the stunned men revived," Doc Savage explained, "and he told us why Oxalate Smith used his invention to murder people and try to get power by extortion, instead of simply selling it to industry for many millions.

"What was the reason?"

"The current has to be changed into static type of electricity before it can be stored," Doc explained. "That makes it commercially useless."

"Useless!"

"There are no practical motors for utilizing static electricity to operate machinery," Doc said. "The condensing invention is worthless commercially."

"That makes me look like a fool, doesn't it?" Annie Spain said. "Even if I didn't know it."

The bronze man frowned. "One thing we have not straightened out—why did he confine his first terrorizing entirely to Smiths?"

"His mind worked that way," the girl explained. "He figured there were enough rich Smiths to start out on. Also, he thought it would help confuse matters."

Monk and Ham, considering that pretty Annie Spain had redeemed herself, renewed their attentions to the young woman. As Long Tom Roberts expressed it, neither Monk nor Ham could tell the difference between a striped tabby cat and a tiger—Annie Spain being tiger caliber, in Long Tom's opinion.

To simplify matters, Monk figured he might persuade Ham to ignore Annie Spain, thus limiting the competition.

Monk accosted Ham. "Ham," he said, "I've discovered a great idea in my head."

"A stowaway," Ham said unkindly.

"I just thought—"

"Yes, I figured so," Ham said. "Let me tell you that each date I have with that girl is like a string of pearls."

"Neckless, my friend, neckless," Monk said. "I've noticed."

And so one word led to another.

DOC SAVAGE

To the world at large, Doc Savage is a strange, mysterious figure of glistening bronze skin and golden eyes. To his fans he is the greatest adventure hero of all time, whose fantastic exploits are unequaled for hair-raising thrills, breathtaking escapes, blood-curdling excitement!

☐	THE EVIL GNOME	2134	$1.25
☐	THE MAN OF BRONZE	6352	$1.25
☐	THE STONE MAN	6419	$1.25
☐	THE BOSS OF TERROR	6424	$1.25
☐	THE THOUSAND HEADED MAN	6471	$1.25
☐	THE RED TERRORS	6486	$1.25
☐	DOC SAVAGE: HIS APOCALYPTIC LIFE	8834	$1.25
☐	THE KING MAKER	10042	$1.25
☐	THE PHANTOM CITY	10119	$1.25
☐	THE MYSTIC MULLAH	10120	$1.25
☐	FEAR CAY	10121	$1.25
☐	LAND OF ALWAYS NIGHT	10122	$1.25
☐	FANTASTIC ISLAND	10125	$1.25
☐	QUEST OF QUI	10126	$1.25

Buy them at your local bookstore or use this handy coupon for ordering:

OUT OF THIS WORLD!

That's the only way to describe Bantam's great series of science-fiction classics. These space-age thrillers are filled with terror, fancy and adventure and written by America's most renowned writers of science fiction. Welcome to outer space and have a good trip!

☐	FANTASTIC VOYAGE by Isaac Asimov	2477	$1.25
☐	STAR TREK: THE NEW VOYAGES by Culbreath & Marshak	2719	$1.75
☐	THE MYSTERIOUS ISLAND by Jules Verne	2872	$1.25
☐	ALAS, BABYLON by Pat Frank	2923	$1.75
☐	A CANTICLE FOR LEBOWITZ by Walter Miller, Jr.	2973	$1.75
☐	RAGA SIX by Frank Lauria	7249	$1.25
☐	THE MARTIAN CHRONICLES by Ray Bradbury	7900	$1.25
☐	HELLSTROM'S HIVE by Frank Herbert	8276	$1.50
☐	HIERO'S JOURNEY by Sterling Lanier	8534	$1.25
☐	DHALGREN by Samuel R. Delany	8554	$1.95
☐	STAR TREK XI by James Blish	8717	$1.75
☐	THE DAY OF THE DRONES by A. M. Lightner	10057	$1.25
☐	THE TOMBS OF ATUAN by Ursula LeGuin	10132	$1.75
☐	20,000 LEAGUES UNDER THE SEA by Jules Verne	10325	$1.25

Buy them at your local bookstore or use this handy coupon for ordering:

THE EXCITING REALM OF STAR TREK

☐ **STAR TREK LIVES!**
　　by Lichtenberg, Marshak & Winston
　　　　　　　　　　　　　　2151　●　$1.95

☐ **STAR TREK: The NEW VOYAGES**
　　by Culbreath & Marshak　　2719　●　$1.75

THRILLING ADVENTURES IN INTERGALACTIC SPACE
BY JAMES BLISH

☐	**SPOCK MUST DIE!**	2245 ●	$1.25
☐	**STAR TREK 1**	2114 ●	$1.25
☐	**STAR TREK 2**	2171 ●	$1.25
☐	**STAR TREK 3**	2253 ●	$1.25
☐	**STAR TREK 4**	2172 ●	$1.25
☐	**STAR TREK 5**	8150 ●	$1.25
☐	**STAR TREK 6**	8154 ●	$1.25
☐	**STAR TREK 7**	2240 ●	$1.25
☐	**STAR TREK 8**	2250 ●	$1.25
☐	**STAR TREK 9**	2238 $	$1.25
☐	**STAR TREK 10**	2241 ●	$1.25
☐	**STAR TREK 11**	8717 ●	$1.25

Bantam Book Catalog

It lists over a thousand money-saving best-sellers originally priced from $3.75 to $15.00 —bestsellers that are yours now for as little as 60¢ to $2.95!

The catalog gives you a great opportunity to build your own private library at huge savings!

So don't delay any longer—send us your name and address and 25¢ (to help defray postage and handling costs).